The Night Visitor

Jeff Hershey

Published by Trellis Publishing, 2021.

THE NIGHT VISITOR

First edition. July 2, 2021.

ISBN: 979-8224727360

Written by Jeff Hershey.

THE NIGHT VISITOR

JEFF HERSHEY

The First Victim

St John's Episcopal was usually dead silent at this time of night, they didn't hold any night services and the weekly meetings were held in the back offices, so the participants normally parked on that side. However, when one of the custodians was doing a walk around to make sure that no trash was discarded near the front steps, they found something much darker. Calls were made, police arrived, and lines were set up to keep curious pedestrians away. A body had been thrown onto the steps, wrapped loosely in a silk sheet, but not clasped shut in any way.

A scene was established, a perimeter secured, and eventually the Detective arrived on scene. Campbell Graves was a seasoned veteran, having served on the police force for almost two decades now he had seen a good number of bad things, but when he arrived at St John's... even seasoned veterans get caught off guard at times. He took a second to walk the perimeter, scope the scene, make sure that the uni's had not missed anything. The victim's profile came through to his phone while he was questioning someone paying to close of attention to the scene. They turned out to be a tabloid reporter looking for a death scoop, Detective Graves had the uni's show the reporter away as he read the profile that came through from the station.

Melanie Womack, age thirty two. A long list of spotty jobs that ended with three S's. Silk/Smooth/Skin, Detective Graves recognized the business name without the profile mentioning anything else. They were a local and mostly reputable porn studio. While SSS didn't offer their actresses enough money or fame to explode onto internet stardom, they did grant enough financial and personal security that something like this shouldn't be able to happen to one of their actresses. SSS did not have a creed or motto that drove them to protect their employees, but more than any other industry they knew that their property was what made them successful.

Melanie's work history had some gaps but knowing the industry she was working in, it wasn't hard to guess the kind of off the books jobs that she would have been filling her time with. She had a sister in East L.A. and a brother in Stockton but other than that her entire family seemed to be spread across the Midwest. Siblings came out here to escape their boring midwest life, it seemed. Detective Graves frowned as he put he phone away after closing the report, he'd found enough steel in his stomach to be able to approach the body again.

Silk sheet, the Detective's eyes lingered on the covering for a bit this time, not because he didn't want to look further. Now that he knew the employment she'd had, he wondered if it was a clue or a jest on the killer's part. Melanie's face was contorted where her head had smacked the stone. She'd been dead so when her jaw broke against the step, it hung loosely with paranormal looking bruising draining down her face from the point of impact. Detective Graves took a quick step away from the body to put on some gloves so that he could avoid contamination.

Once gloved up, Detective Campbell pulled the sheet back to reveal that Melanie was only wearing a white lace bra and a black pencil skirt. Her skin was pale except for her stomach where grotesque red letters carved into her flesh read COME CLEAN.

Detective Graves inspected the carving as detached as possible. The cuts were not clean, they were certainly not surgical in their precision either. They were the block letter equivalent of calligraphy. They were an enraged outcry by an insane person to the victim's soul, demanding that they repent their sins. The Detective covered the body with the sheet and motioned for a pair of uni's to call for the coroner.

As he half-heartedly watched the scene, he tried to get into the mindset of the killer. The silk sheet, the words carved into her stomach, it was clear that the killer knew Melanie. What wasn't clear was the motivation. It could be based in some messed up religion, some out of whack sense of morality, or maybe the killer was more messed up in the head than Detective Graves' first thought. It could have been a personal tragedy that pushed the killer over the edge or some kind of past trauma driving them forward. Hundreds of thousands of people had been hurt by the sex industry, families destroyed and relationships broken. Detective Graves had first hand experience in that regard. His own dalliances had cost him his fiance nearly fifteen years ago now.

Detective Graves revisited on his phone. If the killer knew about her career, then it was not random. He did a quick internet search on the victim's name, nothing came up relating to the victim directly. Her profession did not come up at all, her death was not momentous enough to be discovered already. Diving back into her profile, the Detective found that Melanie had not been on good terms with her brother and sister in California. They knew what she did for a living and according to social media, they refused to talk to her until she sorted her life out. They weren't supportive, but they weren't the killer either. That left one tie back to Melanie's life that could've brought this upon her, SSS. Detective Graves sent a quick message to Morales at the station to get him looking into the company.

There was nothing more to learn at the scene. Detective Graves waited for the coroner to pick up the body and then after making one more pass, he left as well. He had some pent up stress that he needed to work out, the crime scene had done nothing but fuel the fire. As morning crept up around the city, he went to his usual haunt and then fell into a stupor a few hours later in bed with a girl pretending to be a lonely lass. The L's were irrelevant to Detective Graves, might as well take them out because to him she was only ass.

Silk/Smooth/Skin

After the first body was discovered on the steps of St John's Episcopal, Detective Campbell Graves threw his head into the case to no avail. From statements and evidence gathered, despite the fact that she had been alive there was no evidence that she really lived. Her apartment was next to bare, her friends were digital and not more than just barely interested in her life. Everything seemed to revolve around Silk/Smooth/Skin, the porn studio where she was employed. For research purposes, the Detective had gotten his hands on her full catalogue. Just like he had anticipated, she was skilled but there was nothing above and beyond the normal for her industry that would lead to internet fame.

Six days passed, there were no additional leads on the killer, and then another body dropped. Same victimology, same note carved into flesh, same bland life outside of the same career, the only thing different was the church that the body was dropped at. Two bodies in a week, the Captain wanted answers; the Captain wanted to send Detective Graves into SSS studio for answers. As the paperwork was going through, the Detective reviewed previous attempts to investigate crime connected with SSS. None of it had been as heavy as murder, but it all had died at the door. When he reported this to the Captain, it was decided that the Detective would go in undercover to try and suss out the killer.

They were taking their time setting up his identity when the third body dropped. Just like the other two, this girl had nothing special about her life except that she worked for SSS studio. Detective Campbell Graves rushed the request for his cover and when it came back that they just couldn't get to it right now, he pulled the request and went ahead without it. If anyone cared to look that deeply into his past, Campbell figured he could talk out the reason why a Detective was moonlighting at a porn studio. In fact, he realized he could go with the truth, his psychologist was convinced that he was a sex addict.

It was a Friday night when Detective Campbell parked his car across the street from the black and steel modern building with three sleek white S's hanging over the entrance. He took his holstered gun and badge from his belt so that he could stow them away in the glove compartment. His wallet got tucked underneath the driver's seat and he did his best to drop any preconceived notions of what he was walking in to. After all of the work he'd done to research Silk/Smooth/Skin, there was a romantic and sexy credit his mind attributed to the building. When people thought porn studio, they normally imagined one of two things. There was the amateur set up, a guy with a camera filming as the subjects of the film engaged in sloppy and often times uncinematically messy sex.

On the other end of the spectrum, there was the professional side of the industry that had sets of camera jockeys and lighting grips watching as a director guided and gave advice on the scene as one, two or more participants went through the slow and gruelling act of faked pleasure. Silk/Smooth/Skin was somewhere in the middle.

Detective Graves left his car and crossed the street, slipping into a nearly casual demeanor as he opened the door. The lobby was a perfect picture of the studio. To the left there was a shimmering fountain wall, hidden just behind the water was a video scroll that was sensual and sultry. It was hard to tell specifics through the water, but he could make out bare hips swaying in a rhythmic manner. The video paned upward slowly, showing off a bare navel and the bottom of a pair of breasts, before going back downward as the subject spun playfully before settling back into a sensual sway. To the right there were a few waiting chairs, instead of magazines on the end tables there were catalogues of the studio's work. Then, hanging brilliantly in the lighting on the right wall there was a full body image of a blonde woman standing nude with her head thrown back in pleasure. Her left arm covered her nipples, her right hand was cupped between her legs. The picture was clear enough to see the beads of sweat dripping from her flesh, dripping down her stomach.

Directly ahead of him a door opened and a blonde woman sat down behind a glass secretary desk, the Detective approached her with a smile. He hooked a thumb at the picture on the right wall, "That's you, isn't it?"

She looked over at the picture and smiled. Her eyes lazily walked their way back across the lobby before piercing the Detective's soul even from this distance. The way the sun hit her eyes was beautiful but from this distance, he couldn't tell what color they were. She blinked as if to remind him that she were not just art to admire, "What brings you to our studio today?"

"I've got an interview with..." The Detective paused, searching for a good name to guess, but then he settled on, "It's an interview for the security position."

She tilted her head to the side and furrowed her brow. He could tell that she doubted him but he could've never guessed why she didn't believe him, "Are you sure you're here for the position or the contract?"

"Contract?" Detective Graves shook his head slightly. He wasn't sure why the studio would contract security and have regular personnel.

Her face lit up with a wicked grin as she suppressed a laugh. The Detective could tell that he was suddenly on the outside of an inside joke. As if to get the point fully across her eyes lowered down his torso to his trousers and then back up as she slowly said, "The contract position would be on film."

The Detective cleared his throat, that was that last thing he had thought. "Ah. I'm flattered, but unfortunately no. I'm here for the security position."

With the faintest sigh and a slight shrug she replied, "Oh well, the security position is open but the hiring manager is out for the day."

Detective Graves walked up to her desk and stood over her for a moment, "That is a shame."

She smiled and nodded, "Yes, it is. If you want, I could show you around the studio and then you could try back Monday."

Detective Graves smiled and held the prolonged eye contact until it passed from pleasant to slightly awkward to intentional on the part of both parties. "That would be perfect."

"I'll even leave the hiring manager a note... What name should I put down?" She grabbed a pad of sticky notes and a pen without breaking their shared gaze.

"Bell," was all that the Detective answered with.

She wrote without looking and after it was written down, she said, "It's nice to meet you Bell, I'm Emeris. Is there a number I can put down? For the hiring manager."

The Detective gave her his number and then added, "It doesn't have to just be for the hiring manager, you know."

Standing up, Emeris put the sticky note with his information on it in her pocket, "I know."

Now that she was standing just a few feet away from him, the Detective was certain she was the blonde in the picture. Even though she had glossed over the question earlier. "I would love to see some of your work."

Emeris set her hands on her hips as she stepped out from behind the desk, "The studio has a wide collection. I could take you to one of the viewing rooms, though those are typically for investors and partners, not security personnel."

With a shrug of his shoulders, the Detective walked up to Emeris and slipped his hand under her hand on her right hip, "I wasn't talking about the studio."

Emeris laughed softly and leaned up to his ear, "How about I show you to one of our overnight rooms?"

Despite the facade of a tour, the Detective's eyes were transfixed on Emeris's swaying hips as she led him from the lobby to the back of the building. Part of his mind tried to scream out that he was on the job but it was drown in a wave of anticipation and lust as they made their way through the studio. He heard sounds from filming sets as they passed by; every moan he imagined escaping from her lips. He caught a glimpse of flesh through set doors left open; his mind told him it was them intertwined in those sheets.

Finally they went up a flight of steps to a row of one bedroom apartments that Emeris explained were for overworked actors and actresses who did not want to drive home for the night. They were also used for out of town features, but this weekend they were as bare as they normally were. As bare as she wished to be, Emeris had called back to him as she led the way. He barely had a chance to shut the door behind them before her hands found their way to his skin.

Saturday Morning Revelations

The sunlight woke Bell from his slumber, he couldn't remember what time they'd finally fallen asleep, but he could feel the pleasure of the night before as a dull ache in his bones. There was a gentle breeze coming in through the window they'd left open the night before, the sheet was little protection against the cool breeze but Emeris's body pressed up against his was radiating enough warmth that a blizzard could've rolled through and he wouldn't have been able to tell. Rolling over to face his companion, Bell brushed the tangles of blonde hair from her eyes. She stirred softly from her sleep and smiled, "Good morning."

Bell sighed, "I hadn't planned on staying the night when I walked through the door."

Emeris smiled, "Aren't you glad you did, though? I am a professional after all."

With a nod, Bell rolled onto his back, "I am glad."

Bell tried his best to internalize his thoughts so that his companion wouldn't be able to notice. He was supposed to be a professional too, the case strayed into dangerous waters where his weaknesses were concerned. He was on the job, maybe she was too. As if she could sense his thoughts, Emeris broke the silence. "What?"

"You are a professional but are you working?"

Emeris laughed and rolled over onto her back. She was smiling but her laughter stopped as soon as Bell followed after her. A hand on either side of her shoulders as he held himself over her, such a familiar and intimate position. Bell could feel his attention slipping, but he did his best to steel himself and stay on topic. "I'm supposed to believe that I was seduced at a porn studio by one of their best actresses without any interference."

"You can believe whatever you like," Emeris said as her hands ran down his sides before pulling him closer to her. "Would you believe me if I told you it was personal, if I had a long day and just needed... You."

As she said you, Emeris's hand slipped from his back and grabbed on to him. Bell cleared his throat and looked away from her devious smile. Her hand slid up his chest before resting on his check and pulling his eyes back to hers, "Most of us didn't start as actresses. We didn't start in this lavish and well paid lifestyle that you see us in. We started as sex workers and strippers in the most seedy of establishments. It is easy to fake it for the camera when we were already faking it for the Johns."

"If you're trying to help me believe that you weren't faking it earlier, you're not doing a very good job." Bell smiled. He knew that she hadn't been acting earlier.

Emeris furrowed her brow and smirked, "You don't believe me."

"Maybe I don't believe that it's all fake."

"Maybe it isn't, but..." Emeris's voice trailed off as her fingernails dug lightly into Bell's cheek as she looked up toward the head board and shut her eyes as she let out a sensual moan. This close, his body against hers, Bell could feel her writhing beneath him. As soon as it began, he knew that it was an imitation. They had experienced the real thing together, maybe that was why he could tell, but as Emeris heaved her chest he felt himself drawn to her again.

When he tried to look down at her naked form, Emeris's fingers held his eyes locked to her face as she bit her lip and bucked her hips against his. Her moans grew louder and the passion within her stirrings rose with every passing second. Bell felt himself boiling over but just before he lost all will to stay still, Emeris halted her act and opened her eyes. The blood returned to her cheeks and she gave him that same wicked smirk she had toyed him with earlier. Emeris removed her fingernails from his cheek and slipped out from under him, "I'm hungry. How about we get dressed and head out for breakfast?"

"If we have to." Bell joked.

"I don't think anyone would mind if we didn't," Emeris answered seriously and then with a smile added, "though I think that some of my coworkers might try to steal you away from me if you walk around like that."

After they dressed, Bell drove them a few miles away to a good breakfast spot that Emeris suggested. It was quaint, especially for the area it was in, but it was busy enough that no one bothered them but slow enough that they had time to sit down and really dive in to their meal. The conversation built slowly, Bell was hesitant to say much about himself because he didn't know how much he could give away without tipping his hand about the true intentions he had for going to the studio.

Emeris was an open book for him to read through, she was forthcoming with her answers and she answered with a certain blunt honesty to every question that Bell had been missing for a while. She was not giving away her life story, they did not delve into her past at all, but when they talked about beliefs, politics, and entertainment inclinations, Bell was surprised by how much their ideals aligned. Not only was she beautiful, not only was she as erotic as could be, not only was she interested in Bell beyond just the bedroom antics they'd gotten up to, but she was more in tune with him than anyone else had been in a long time. As they ate breakfast, Bell found himself realizing that it wasn't just a happy combination of infatuation and lust that he was feeling for Emeris. The stirrings in his heart were ancient and nearly forgotten, but he remembered what love felt like. If only because he had felt it once before and heard about it so often since then.

When the meal dove to a close, Bell realized that he failed to grab his wallet from the car. Emeris volunteered to grab it for him and in the rush of the night before as well as this morning, he told her to check the glove box for it. She came back a few moments later with some cash he'd had tucked inside the fold of his badge, for when forgot his wallet. Bell realized what happened as soon as he saw her walking back in, there was nothing different about her demeanor and it was as if the revelation meant nothing to her. She handed him the money, he paid for the meal, and then they left together.

Once they were back at the studio, Bell broke the silence on the topic, "So, I guess you know what I do for a living."

Emeris shrugged, "I figured as much. Not many people with that look work security. It was either cop or soldier, my money was on cop. Why? Does it change anything between us?"

Between us. The way she said it made Bell's mind shatter for a moment. As he put the pieces back together, he smiled, "Not as far as I'm concerned."

"Good." Emeris led the way in to the lobby.

There was a brunette behind the secretary's desk now. She looked up when they came through the door, her face was covered in sorrow. It wasn't an expression Bell had expected to see, "What's wrong?"

The words left his mouth before he'd known he wanted to say them. The brunette turned the computer screen so that they could see it as they approached, "They found another body. It's Carly."

On the screen there was a picture of a young girl, she was smiling and as soon as Bell saw her smile, he felt his own disappear completely. There was a sudden familiarity about her and even though Emeris and the brunette were talking to each other, Bell couldn't hear them. He was pulled back into his own memory, less than a decade ago he had hired the girl for a few hours in a back alley just a few blocks from where he stood now.

There was nothing special about her, he barely even remembered their encounter. It had been quick and dirty, then he paid her before they went their separate ways. The only reason that he remembered her at all was that he'd hired her the same day that his wife had handed him the papers for their divorce. They'd been separated for a while but it had been longer since Bell had been spending his spare time with prostitutes in alleys and motel rooms. This girl was not the first and she had not been the last, but she had been a moment of pleasure in a sea of confusion for Bell.

Emeris's hand rested on his shoulder, bringing him back, "Are you okay?"

Bell nodded, "Yeah. You never asked if I was on the job when we talked earlier."

Emeris sighed, "Should I have?"

"I asked you."

Emeris chuckled, "Would it change anything between us if you were?"

"Not for me." Bell shook his head, "But I'm here about these killings."

"Ah." was all that Emeris said. She wasn't smiling, but Bell could tell that she wasn't upset or confused. She understood even though he hadn't really explained. He liked that about her.

"I need to know if there was a connection here between the four victims." Bell asked as he realized the brunette had left and it was just Emeris with him now.

She sat down behind the desk and swiveled the computer back to where she could type easily. After a few moments of clacking keys, Emeris shook her head, "Even though they were all young and relatively the same body type, none of them worked together. Carly and Melanie have strictly heterosexual contracts, Priscilla and Taren on the other hand are into some... pretty taboo stuff in very different directions from each other. No reason any of them would've worked together."

Bell sighed, "Is there any chance I can take a look at their things?"

Emeris frowned, "We all do have lockers here and I can give you their combinations..."

"But?" Bell asked.

Emeris smirked, "But I'm not sure if I'm supposed to just give that over to a lawman. What would be in it for me? I would be going against company policy."

Bell sighed, "I know, I know you're not supposed to hand it over, but that's four bodies in less than two weeks. I need to find this guy. Sorry, I'm not really in the mindset for bribery, even if it is the well intentioned and sexy kind."

Emeris set her hand on Bell's and smiled softly. Her eyes lost their devious glint and she truly looked apologetic as she said, "I'm sorry I know the timing is bad but I thought you were sexy before I knew that you had a pair of handcuffs, now I'm just thinking of all the other things we could do together now. I'll call my boss, she won't answer because she's off this weekend but I'll leave a message about it and then play dumb if it isn't okay with it on Monday."

"Thank you."

"What else would a pornstar paramour be good for?" Emeris smiled as she stood up from the desk and squeezed Bell's hand. "That is what we are now, aren't we? I know you can feel it between us. Unless you want me for more than just sex."

"I want more. I feel more than that. There's more that you don't know, though." Bell admitted.

Emeris came up closer to him and put her hands on his chest, "What could you tell me that would change how I'm feeling?"

"About ten years ago I hired a prostitute on a late night for a quick romp in my car. I've done it quite a few times... but that night it was Carly. I didn't know her name at the time, but I remember her face."

Emeris didn't pull away, "She must've been something."

"She was nothing." Bell shook his head and took a step back from Emeris, "She was stress relief the night my wife divorced me."

Emeris grabbed Bell's hand again and pulled him back to her, "When are you going to get to the part where I have to look at you differently? You've hired a prostitute or two in your time, but that doesn't mean much to me. I'm a porn star, I've alluded to what I used to do for a living if not blatantly hinted at it. Why would that bother me."

"I'm not sure..." Bell took a deep breath, "I'm not sure about all four of them, but I know that I'm the connection between Carly and Taren. Melanie and Priscilla looked familiar but I can't remember if I hired them or if I've just been looking at their pictures for the case for so long that I feel familiar with them."

"Are you admitting serial murder right now?" Emeris let go of Bell's hand and backed away. Her eyes suddenly full of surprise with hints of fear.

Bell shook his head, "I slept with them years ago. I haven't even thought of them consciously since them. What I'm afraid of, what I think might push you away is that someone is killing them to highlight me. I know it's a long shot, that's why I want to look at their things, to find another connection. Something that connects them all to someone or something other than me, other than this studio."

Emeris smiled a weary and heavy smile, "So you're worried that because we slept together last night that I'll become another body to throw at your feet? What did you do that you need to come clean on? Just the prostitutes?"

Bell shook his head, "I'm not afraid because of last night, I'm afraid because I am falling in love with you. I'm not afraid that someone will use you against me, I'm afraid that I will lose you."

Emeris smiled, Bell had held something back and he was certain that she could tell. She didn't press him further, instead she wrapped her fingers in between his and lead him back to the employee locker room. Bell suppressed a laugh when they arrived, it was a locker room for sure. An exact replica of a high school locker room down to the tile floors and the communal shower in the corner, there were also five or seven cameras set up and set lights hanging up above. Emeris smiled and moved a camera out of her way as she led Bell to the victim's lockers, "Why not take advantage of the space afforded by this set?"

Bell finally lost his hold over his laughter and had to shake his head, "That's not why I'm laughing."

"Why then?"

"I'm pretty sure I've seen some of your work before." Bell pointed to the communal shower, "I seem to recall you were one of several cheerleaders in a... ah... wet and wild video online."

Emeris shrugged, "I love a good cheerleader outfit."

"If I'm remembering correctly, I loved you in that outfit."

Emeris smiled as she stopped in front of a locker and looked back at Bell with that devious smirk, "This one was Carly's. Not to distract from the task at hand, but if you ever want to see that outfit again, just let me know. As an actress, I have all of my costumes stored here for future use. That is unless they get destroyed as a part of a scene."

As she turned back to the locker, Emeris bent over so that she could start to put the combination in. Admiring her from behind, Bell struggled to keep his mind on topic, especially when Emeris added quietly, "or if they get destroyed for personal use."

Suspect Identified

Detective "Bell" Graves was relieved when Emeris came up with a connection between the victims that didn't involve him in the slightest. According to their lockers, they all had appointments on their calendars for the day before their murder with the same person. In the case of Carly and Taren, Emeris was able to confirm with others at the studio that heading to that appointment was the last time anyone had seen the actresses. It seemed that the Detective finally found a credible suspect in Jamie Galloway. According to some detailed notes that Melanie had taken before going to her appointment, Jamie Galloway was a talent scout for a larger porn studio that was interested in hiring on new talent for short term, well paying contracts. To the actresses, it must've sounded like a dream. Knowing how they ended up though, Bell and Emeris could only see it as a trap. However, once the name had come up, they hit two roadblocks that the Detective didn't see coming.

The first was that Jamie Galloway was supposed to be dead, at least according to the police database that the Detective relied on to be able to do his job. There was no photo on the file that the station sent to his phone, not even a description. The only entry was that a sister had reported him missing and he was presumed dead. There was next to no information about Mr. Galloway in the file, but there was a listed address. It was shockingly close to the studio and when cross referenced against the actresses' schedules, it was the last address they had listed. The second thing to snag up Bell's attention was that Emeris had the same name written down in her calendar. She was supposed to meet with Galloway tonight, at the address the other girls had gone to, and now that she realized the similarity in her life and the other victims, she was sure that she would be next. After promises that she would not be next, Bell left her behind at the studio with a protective detail as he headed for the apartment. As he didn't have a partner, Bell put in a call for a squad car to back him up.

Bell was posted across the street from the address in the victim's calendars. From the comfort of his car, he watched as a six foot tall man moved about the house as if cleaning up or looking for something. Jamie's file was surprisingly light, Bell had no way to be sure that the man was his suspect. With Emeris's safety hanging in the balance, Bell only saw that there was no way to be sure it wasn't his suspect either. Who else would be rifling through the house of someone missing for months? It wasn't the sister that put in the missing persons report. As Bell waited, he sent a note back to the station to look into the officer that filed out the report, it was criminally bare in regards to necessary information.

When word came down that the car was thirty minutes out, Bell started to stress. The suspect, Galloway, could go anywhere in thirty minutes. Bell could only keep an eye on him as long as he stayed in the front of the house. When the squad car reported that they hit traffic and were still two miles out, Bell couldn't sit still. The man inside the house stepped out the side door, dumped a black trash bag into his garbage bin, and then went back inside. To Bell's dismay, the man went to the back of the house and Bell lost sight of him.

That was as long as Bell could stand to wait. The moment the man left his sight, Bell was out of his car and crossing the street. His hand on the grip of his holstered gun, Bell charged up the steps to the front door and pounded it furiously, "LAPD open up!"

He heard a crash, the man was running. Bell shouted again and then he heard the side door burst open. Bell went around the side of the house on but got their just in time to catch a glimpse of his suspect rounding the far corner as the side door lazily hung open. Bell had no way to identify him, chasing after would do no good. The only thing Bell could do was clear the house and make sure that it had actually been his suspect fleeing. Drawing his gun, Bell called out as he stepped through the threshold into the house, "LAPD! If there is anyone in this house, identify yourself!"

No one answered. Bell kept his eyes and ears open as he moved from room to room, he radioed the squad car to see how far out they were. There was no response. Bell made it a few more steps before something hit him hard in the back of the head and he fell like a sack of potatoes.

Graves and Galloway

Bell woke in a chair, hands tied behind his back with rope. There was a single light over head, swaying slightly from side to side. His head was swimming, his vision was spotty, but despite all of that, he forced himself to stay focused as best he could. There was a man standing in front of him, the man from the house Bell was certain. He was holding Bell's gun in one hand and his badge in the other. The man chuckled, "Detective Campbell Graves... What am I going to do with you?"

"Kill me or let me go." Bell said quickly, his head hurt. He did not feel like chatting it up with a murderer.

The man chuckled again, he was amused. Maybe it was a power trip for him, maybe that was why he killed those girls. He replied, "Why would I kill you?"

"You killed those girls."

The man grabbed Bell by his short hair and wrenched his head upward. The part that caught Bell off guard was that he was certain the man had just been several feet away. The pain was nothing next the throbbing in Bell's head. Bell tried to pull away but it was no use, the man had a firm grip on his hair.

He twisted Bell's head so that Bell had to look up at him, "Do you know who I am?"

"You're Jamie Galloway." Bell spit at his captor, or at least tried to but it fell short onto Bell's own lap. Regardless of the miss, Bell's captor let go of his hair and took a step back.

Bell's answer seemed to amuse the captor, he chuckled deeply and then shook his head. The ropes at Bell's wrist had felt so secure when he first woke, but now they felt slack. Before his captor could say anything, Bell slipped his hands free. One hand grabbed his gun back while his other hand pushed his captor away.

They were both standing now, six or so feet apart. Bell's captor had his hands raised in surrender, Bell had the gun squared off at his heart. "Why did you kill those girls?"

The man smiled, "Come clean."

Bell took a step closer, "What the fuck does that mean? You come clean! Why did you kill those girls?"

The man shook his head, "I don't think you understand. The message wasn't for them. It was for you. Come clean, Campbell Graves."

"I have nothing to-" Bell stopped as the man's gaze intensified. Bell had the gun but he felt powerless.

After a moment of silence, the man spoke up. "She had a family. Come clean."

Bell was horrified. He had done everything right, he had cleaned it all up, he made sure that there was no world in which his mistake would splash back on him. His will was broken, even though he tried to muster a lie, he couldn't manage to sound convincing, "I don't know what you're talking about. Why did you kill those girls?"

The man's response made everything real, "Why did you kill Jamie Galloway?"

Bell had never known her name, only that she was a prostitute and that he needed some quick release. He had been getting increasingly violent with the girls he hired. It had all started with Taren, she had been so insistent that he hit her while they fucked that Bell finally let go and smacked her as hard as he could on the cheek. Her cheek turned red instantly, her eye watered and a line of blood dribbled from her nose. Then she begged for more. It had all started with that, Bell thought he had a handle on it, he had it under control. Until the night that he went too far with a girl he picked up down by the docks. At the time she had seemed into it but after meeting Emeris, Bell wondered if it was all an act. If it was just her playing for him, but it didn't matter. Bell choked her with both hands and it drove him to a climax. Her neck had snapped like a twig in his hands. After it happened, after he cleaned it up, he had watched the news, the reports, and the headlines at work. No one found the body, no one came looking for her. Bell had thought he was free and clear.

Bell pressed the gun against his persecutor's chest, "What the hell do you know?"

Even with a gun pressed to his chest, the man smiled, "I know that Jamie had a sibling that loved her more than anything else in the world. I know that when Jamie died that sibling lost everything. I know that the sibling threw themselves into Jamie's case to no avail, there was no body and no proof and while Jamie had never been arrested or picked up for solicitation, the officer that looked into the missing person's report didn't even bother once they figured it out. No one cares about a missing prostitute. Is that what you thought when you disposed of her body?"

Bell exhaled deeply from his nose, he couldn't lose his temper. He couldn't lose control, this man knew nothing. Despite that, knew somewhere in his mind that this was the end. He pushed the man away with the barrel of his gun, putting some distance between them.

Bell cleared his throat and asked, "What do you want? Money? An apology? Would you even forgive me? I'm sorry I killed your sister but she is gone. She meant nothing to no one and you're never going to be able to prove that I'm the one that snapped her neck."

Something changed in the man's eyes, Bell had seen it before and he knew what was coming next. Instead of letting the man charge him, Bell pulled the trigger twice and plugged two bullets into his persecutor's chest. His momentum carried him forward even though he hadn't taken a proper step, he fell to the ground on his chest and lay there. Bell sighed, it was over. It was time to figure out where he was and get away from here. Even if the man couldn't prove anything, it was time for him to leave L.A. with Emeris at his side.

As he took a step back toward the chair he'd been sitting in, he spotted a red light in the darkness just before a barrage of light assaulted him. He was disoriented, he stumbled, but when he blinked his eyes found himself in a room painted a dull concrete gray. There were two racks of lights on the ceiling, production lighting not standard lights. There were four professional film cameras staged around the room. There were no windows and only one door, the door was open and Emeris stood defiantly in the doorway, a relieved look on her face.

Emeris smiled, "Jamie didn't have a brother."

Bell cursed and aimed the gun at Emeris. He pulled the trigger and it bucked realistically in his hands, but no bullet tore through the air. Emeris smiled and something struck Bell in the back of the head, knocking him unconscious to the ground. Emeris stood defiant over her sister's killer and smiled, "Javier, you can leave the tape here with him. Lock the door after you properly tie him up for the police. I'll make sure to wire you the second half of your fee by the end of the day."

"Sure thing, Ms. Galloway."

SHIT HOLE

MARY SAVAGE

Chapter One

He'd spent five years in that hellhole before he made an informed decision: prison fucking sucks. He spent the majority of his day locked in a cell with some psychopath that claimed to hear voices in his head telling him to do crazy shit like wear his underwear on his head or punch that big guy, Stone, in the yard. Stone had nearly killed the poor bastard, but Joe Sullivan, aka "Sully" here, didn't give two shits about him. Not when he ate something gray that might have once been meat for breakfast, lunch, *and* dinner and drank water with a yellowish tint to it. Not when he slept on mattresses lumpier than the alley floors he used to sleep on as a kid, when his mother was jobless and they had no place to call home. Not when he had these assholes who call themselves correctional officers screaming in his ear like they're talking to some old deaf guy and shoving him around like it's some kind of game.

So many times he's wanted to retaliate, to bash their heads in, to slit their throats with a handmade shank, to slap their own cuffs onto their wrists and beat them mercilessly with their own nightsticks. But he was smarter than that; he knew that were he to so much as pluck a single hair from any guard's head, there would be consequences. Namely, more time added on to his sentence and even harsher punishment from the dickheads within the prison itself; the very same ones that were supposed to be protecting him from his other cell mates.

But the very worst part about all of this shit was the fact that he hadn't even done anything wrong to deserve it—well, at least not what they *thought* he'd done.

He's not going to lie; he's wasted a few traitors to the gang. More than one man is buried six feet under with his trademark cigarette burn on the back of the neck, but he swears on his mother's grave that he never even went near that chick they're saying he offed. He didn't even recognize her name, but apparently she was some rich bitch daughter of a senator or something. Raped and killed and dumped in an alley about a mile away from his house, a cigarette burn on the back of her neck and a threatening letter—supposedly from him—found in the pocket of her designer coat.

The police had barely even had to prove his guilt. He was so well-known in this city, by all the jurors and the deliberation had taken less than a minute before he was found Guilty of all crimes. He was sentenced to 20-Life and sent upstream. His girl, Pat, visited him sometimes and they used Morse taps to communicate as they chatted about mundane subjects like the weather and sports games he couldn't give two shits about.

Through their taps, he found out about the man who framed him, Rick Silas, who'd once been his friend, but was now a bitter rival. Rick and Joe had had a falling out years ago over something as absurd as splitting their shares from a lifted purse. There was only about a hundred dollars in the damn thing and Rick's argument was that, since he's the one who distracted the old lady in the first place, he should get a bigger split. Joe fought that it should be equal, since they both did their part in the theft. They'd fought like animals afterwards and one sock in the jaw had Rick backing off.

"Keep it, you greedy fuck!" he roared. "I'll find my own!" It had been a year until he saw Rick again and by that time he already had his own operation going. And Rick was never one to let go of grudges easily.

Cops starting inexplicably hanging around Joe's house, where he, Pat, and their own group of 'outlaws' lived. They sold drugs, stole drugs, used persuasive tactics—such as wielding a knife or a gun—to get their own way, and sold knockoffs. With the cops watching their place, Joe had to be ten times as careful, warding off the fuzz with his natural charm and power of persuasion. He fucked more than one female cop while Pat gave blowjobs to the majority of the males. They weren't bothered at all until the rich bitch turned up dead.

When the cops came to his door then, they didn't even ask questions before shoving a warrant in his face and slapping cuffs on him. At the time, Joe had no idea what he'd done or who had accused him but he already swore revenge as they shoved him into the back of a police car. Nobody wanted to listen to him plead his innocence and his trial was set for the following month, at the senator's insistence.

To find out that it was Rick was no big surprise, but he cursed out loud nonetheless, causing two of the guards to look his way.

"It's supposed to rain tomorrow," he lied and they looked away, uncaring.

It was then that he started to plan his revenge, meeting with Pat every few weeks to tap it out. She informed them that half of their guys had gone over to Rick's side when Joe went away, that they were now loyal to him and they were missing half of their manpower. Nobody had discovered the drug ring, but people were wary about buying from them now that their leader was away. Rick had done all of this, the prick. He would pay.

Now it was five years later and still there was no way to put their plan into action without Joe there to guide them. Pat was persuasive, but she was no gang leader, that was for damn sure. She was just his right hand; the person who echoed his orders and pointed a gun at whoever wavered. She was loyal and tough, but not tough enough for what he had in mind.

He was being driven insane every single day as he listened to his roommate mutter to himself, his head banging a rhythm against the wall. The only thing that kept him going anymore was the thirst for revenge. And Ann's letters.

Ann was another rich bitch. But she hadn't known the victim too well, except for the rumors she heard about the girl's tryst with some gang member. She was the first to write to him and tell him that she believed he was innocent. She wrote, in her first letter, that the gang member the girl was associated with was black, not white like Joe, and lived on the other side of the city—at least according to the rumors she'd heard. She'd tried to tell the cops that but none of them had listened. As far as they were concerned, she was just another little heiress looking for attention.

But the fact that somebody outside his own group thought he was innocent was enough to make Joe respond to that first letter—and then every letter thereafter. Their correspondence lasted for the entirety of his time in prison and he kept every single letter in his pillowcase, smiled when they crinkled at night as he rolled over. He didn't tell Pat about the letters.

He received one on the day his plans would be set into motion.

"Dear Joe,

Since receiving your last letter, I've been thinking a lot about what I would like to do for the rest of my life and I've decided that I'm going to go for it. I'm going to tell my father about my art, show him my paintings. Maybe he'll understand, you know? Maybe he won't be mad at all. I mean, I'm his daughter and he loves me, doesn't he? Won't he just be happy that I'm happy? I'm sure he will and so I'm going to tell him. Better late than never, after all. Right?

And Joe, I don't think I've ever asked you want you want to be. As in your career? I know it'll be a while before you can even consider it, but what is it that you've always wanted to do with your life? Something besides a life of crime, I mean, though to each his own I guess. Let me know in your next letter. I'll be looking forward to it.

Sincerely, Ann Martin"

It was shorter than most of his letters but he tucked it away into the inner coat of his jacket anyway. He would answer no more letters but he wouldn't leave them here, where psycho could get his hands on them. And, besides, having them closer to him made him feel safer as he made his way into the yard, where hundreds of other inmates stood, talking and just taking in the short amount of fresh air they were allotted each day.

Joe strolled casually through the crowds, down a familiar trail, his eyes skating over the faces of guards and his fellow inmates, many of whom were watching him. Platt, a lifer whose cell was located three down from Joe's gave him a hard glance and Joe smirked, held up two fingers, and walked further down the path, approaching the fence. He stopped and sat on the ground, closing his eyes as he counted backwards from a hundred and twenty. At five, his eyes opened again, just in time to see Platt punch Linster in the jaw. This was followed by Brown, another inmate, who sat with Joe at most meals, kneeing some unknown Latino in the groin.

Joe watched as the entire yard dissolved into chaos. The guards all around the yard ran straight towards the mess of inmates fighting one another, throwing punches and kicks and attacking one another with clawed hands. He smiled and reveled in the beauty of it before turning on his head and continuing down the path. Nobody even looked his way.

At the edge of the yard, about a quarter mile away from the entrance into the prison, there was a weak spot of fence. It wasn't electric, for safety reasons, but barbed wire ran all over its length and height—except here. Here, there was a noticeable gap in the barbs, where they split and were easily moved away to reveal a hole in the fence itself. When Joe had first noticed it, after taking a few laps around the sparse yard, there had been no way he could fit through it. It was too small even for the slender Pat to fit through.

But five years, fifty pounds less, and a bit of digging with a hundred or so easily broken plastic spoons, and the hole he made just underneath it might allow him a not-so-easy exit. This was his only chance at escape, either way. He had traded all his belongings to Platt and Brown for their little stunt. Platt didn't take too much convincing but Brown wasn't a lifer and had demanded almost more than Joe could give.

It proved worth it when Joe got down on his knees and slid through the hole like a slithering snake. Maybe he'd lost more weight than he thought in that shithole. He'd have to find a way to make it back after he got settled and wasted that dirtbag of an ex-partner, Rick.

He stood, brushed himself off, and then ran, never looking over his shoulder. The street was just a few hundred yards away and Pat would be waiting for him there, her trunk already open for him to jump into, a bag of fresh clothes for him to change into. She always had him covered, his Pat.

By the time he reached the car, he figured they must be looking for him so he wasted no breath to say hello or thank her for what she was doing. He just jumped into the trunk, shut it, and rolled around as she drove off. But he didn't really care about how sore his muscles were or what a close call he might have just had because he was free.

He was finally fucking free.

Chapter Two

There was absolutely no way they could return to his old house. For one thing, that would have been the first place they looked for him, and for another...well, since his incarceration and the whole operation going belly up and everything, they'd been forced to sell it.

"We got everything out, though," she told him as they walked into the new safe house, located about twenty miles from the city, in the middle of a large wooded area. It had belonged to Pat's late father, used only for fishing and cheating on her mother with his skanks. "It's all here, in the basement. The boys are out on the streets with it right now."

"How do they get back and forth?" Joe asked, always worried about his boys. He tugged his jeans up his hips; they were too big for him now.

"I drive them," Pat told him. "And Jimmy's got a good car now, too."

"Jimmy's sixteen," Joe snorted, looking around the tiny, damp living room.

"Not anymore," Pat said, tugging his hand as she moved towards the couch. "He's got a girl and a kid now. He's got a job down at the docks."

"And he's still selling?"

"He's still loyal. Besides, he ain't making enough to support his family with that dock shit; he needs the cash so I try to help him out, you know." Pat pushed him down onto the couch and climbed up onto his lap, smiling down on him like the Cheshire cat. "Let's not talk about it now, though, alright? We got more important things to do." She began to press kisses against his neck, smiling against his skin as he planted his hands on her hips.

"Pat, babe, we shouldn't—" he started but she pulled back and placed one finger against his lips to silence him.

"We've got plenty of time to do other shit, Joey," she said, "but you've been locked up for half a decade; surely there's something you missed in that time, huh? A bit more, uh, *pressing* issue." She palmed him and he groaned. "See? Now just sit back and relax; Patti's got it all covered, baby."

He was too distracted to argue further.

They lay in bed after three full rounds of what could barely be called sex. It was more like Pat had pounced on him, doing 90% of the work while he just lay there, reaping the benefits. The bed in the master bedroom was ten times as comfortable as the old prison mattress and he found himself starting to drift off as Pat lay against him, catching him up on everything that had happened since their last prison visit.

"...and he got that Martin girl all tied up somewhere in his house. Also, Jimmy's girl is pregnant again with a—"

"Wait," Joe interrupted. "What did you say? About the Martin girl? You mean *Ann*?"

"Yah, I think that's 'er name. Why? You know her?" Pat asked, looking up at him.

Joe nodded as he sat up, dislodging Pat. "Yeah," he said. "she, ah, wrote to me. In prison."

"She's one of *those* chicks?" Pat laughed. "Crazy ass women fallin' for convicts who'd sooner kill them than—"

"You sayin' I'm a murderer, Pat?" Joe barked, startling her.

"'Course not, Joey," she assured him. "I mean, I know you killed people, but those bastards always had it comin', didn't they? So it's all good. I'm just saying *she* didn't know that, is all."

Joe took a deep breath and rubbed the back of his neck. "I know what you're sayin'," he said. "But Ann didn't think I was guilty. She said I must've been framed 'cause I didn't match the description of the girl's boyfriend. Apparently, he was in a gang too."

"Did she say which?" Ann asked, sitting up to rest on her knees next to him.

Joe nodded. "It was Rick's, obviously," he said. "We know that. Poor girl was probably lured in and murdered in cold blood."

"Not before they got their way with her I'll bet," Pat huffed. "Poor...what was her name again?"

"Something Grant, I don't fuckin' know," Joe sighed. "Point is, he killed that poor girl just to get back at me and now he's gonna kill Ann, too. 'Less we do somethin' about it."

"Which we are," Pat reminded him. "In just a few short weeks, we're gonna infiltrate his place and—"

"We don't have weeks, Patti," Joey growled, throwing the sheets off of his legs and standing. He grabbed his boxers and began pulling his clothes on. "We don't even have a few days. You know Rick; he'll play with his new little toy for a few days and then he'll get bored, shoot her dead, and bury her in the backyard." He shook his head. "I've seen him do it too many times and I ain't about to let another girl die on my account."

"So what do you wanna do, then?" Pat asked, following him out of the room, a sheet wrapped around her naked body. "Just storm in there with no backup *tonight*? He's got a million guys in that house of his; ain't no way we're gonna take them all down, just the two of us."

"He won't be keeping her in his house, anyway," Joe dismissed. "He's too smart for that. 'Specially since that girl's daddy is probably lookin' everywhere for her right at this very moment. No, he's keepin' her somewhere, but wh—" His eyes widened as he looked back at Pat. "Is Sabretooth still around?"

"You mean Rick's bitch?" Pat snorted humorlessly, shaking her head, dirty blonde locks shaking with the motion. "'Course he is. But you don't think…" Joe grinned. "Rick wouldn't keep that girl with Sabe; he's a twice-convicted rapist. He couldn't expect the perv to resist somebody like that."

"You said it yourself; Sabretooth is Rick's bitch; whatever he says, that dumbass does. Rick probably distracted him with a couple dozen of his own hoes, anyhow." He paused to take a breath. "Where's he livin' now, Sabretooth. He still got that house on Seventh?"

"Far as I know," Pat said. "I haven't spoken to the bastard in years, but I don't really see any reason for him to change his address; he's been out of jail eight years now. Supposedly, he's doing good, despite more allegations coming up on the contrary." She shook her head. "Even if Sabe *does* have the Martin girl, do you know how hard it's gonna be to bring down all *his* goons? We're gonna need at least a half dozen of our guys and I don't think they'll be up for something like that tonight, babe."

"First light, then," Joe said. "We'll leave when the sun rises; make sure everybody's got their shit together."

"Sweetheart," Pat replied, "I'm loyal to you; you know I am. But I ain't no miracle worker and those boys haven't had their shit together since they was in diapers."

Chapter Three

By morning, all but three of Joe's main group of men had arrived back to Pat's safehouse. Jimmy, Sam, and Teddy were all family men now, which surprised Joe but he wasn't about to take them away from what they'd all worked so hard to gain.

Besides, even without them he still had more than a dozen guys ready to help him take Sabretooth down. Sabe had been one of them once, before Rick had betrayed them all. It hadn't taken the bastard a week to pack up all his shit and run to Rick's side, though. Joe hadn't even been surprised—nor did he care, considering Sabretooth was a lousy shot and proved to be a double-crosser, anyway. Who needed him?

Thankfully, all the men that stayed knew Sabe well enough to know all his tells and his strengths and weaknesses and how fucking dumb that man got when anything in a skirt showed up. He thought with his dick and that was a fatal flaw that made Joe burst into random bouts of laughter. His boys followed.

The plan was simple: Their three strongest—Bo, Gabe, and Devon—would lead the group. Being the muscle meant that they'd be able to easily take out any shitheads guarding around the house and allow the rest to get in. Behind them were about six of Joe's most weapon-savvy men; TJ, Mart, Steve, Bardy, Paulie, and Fisher. Their weapons were, for the most part, concealed by their clothing, but easily accessible when they needed them. They would enter the house before Pat, Joe, and the rest, guns blazing as they took out anyone on the first floor (though they were warned to be way of any blonde girls who looked as if they might be scared or mistreated.) Once they cleared, Joe and Pat would lead the others upstairs, where Ann was most likely be held. He knew, from experience, that there were only three possible rooms she could be held in, so they would be split into partners. He and Pat would be together, of course.

"This girl really that important to you?" Dove, the only other female gang member asked as they waited for the all-clear from Bardy. "I wouldn't even go that far for a piece of ass."

"She ain't a piece of ass, Dove," Joe snapped. "She's an innocent. And the only person who believed me when she didn't have to. We don't let people like that die on our watch, alright?"

"Okay, okay," Dove muttered. "Damn."

"Clear!" Bardy called out to Joe and he lead them out from the gathering of bushes they'd been hiding in, each pulling out their weapons as they approached the house. Joe took the safety off his Glock as he immediately started up the stairs. Pat was on his heel. At the top of the stairs, they split into their groups. Dove went with Stu, and Bardy would search another room with TJ, while Pat and Joe took the last room.

"You ready for this?" Pat asked him. "You might not like what you see. She might already be dead."

"I'll hate myself if I don't make sure," Joe responded. "So, yes. I'm ready."

"Fingers crossed." Pat kicked in the door, her gun pointed inside.

The room was completely empty, but for a few chairs and boxes, and three people. The first was the man himself; Sabretooth was a slimy man with a shark's tooth necklace around his neck. He was skinny and tall and his breath constantly stank of onions. It was no wonder he had to stoop as low as rape to get any action. Just the very sight of him made Joe's stomach lurch; he was sickening.

Behind him was a scantily clad, brown-skinned woman with firetruck-red short hair that hung over her eyes in a fringe. She barely even glanced their way, too distracted by the tiny blonde she had her arms wrapped around, her lips attached to the pulse point of a visibly uncomfortable young woman.

Ann. That was Joe's Ann. The same woman who's scrawling cursive he'd read at least twice a week since he was sent away. Her dress was torn and her makeup was smudged and her hair looked like a rat's nest, but there was no mistaking the woman in all the pictures she'd sent him over the years. Only the woman in the pictures was constantly smiling; there was no trace of a smile on her face her. Not even when he could clearly read the look recognition on her face. Instead, he looked absolutely terrified.

"What did you do to her?" Joe barked at Sabe, who just grinned in return.

"Hey to you, too, Joey; how've you been?" he responded. "How was prison?"

"What did you do to her?" Joe repeated, completely ignoring the other man's questions.

"Me?" Sabe asked, as if offended. "Absolutely nothing. My girl, Lourdes, however..."

"GET YOUR HANDS OFF OF HER!" Joe boomed, his gun pointing in the woman's direction. She didn't even blink.

"Don't be ridiculous," Sabretooth laughed. "She knows you won't do anything while she'd wrapped around your girl. Lourdes may be a hoe, but she ain't stupid." He laughed again and pulled his own gun. "I, however, don't care about either bitch." He pointed his gun at them and finally Lourdes stopped, her eyes going wide.

"Sabe?" she asked, stepping away from Ann, who fell to the floor in a fit of sobs. Sabretooth wasted no time in shooting her through the school. Lourdes's body fell to the floor as blood gushed from the wound in her head and Ann screamed. Sabretooth pointed the gun at her next and she began to beg and plead for her life.

"He won't hurt you," Joe told her. "He can't."

"The fuck you mean, I can't?" Sabretooth hissed, his gun trained on Ann's head. "You've seen me shoot bitches before, haven't you? Or have you forgotten?"

"I haven't forgotten what a little bitch you are," Joe said, taking a step forward. Sabe's gun swung around to point at him.

"The fuck you say to me?" he growled. "I ain't no bitch."

Joe scoffed. "Of course you are," he said. "You were my bitch for years and then you left me to be Rick's bitch. And no bitch of Rick's is about to kill his favorite toy; not if he don't wanna be killed in return. Trust me, Sabe, you're a total bitch."

"You wanna see a bitch, motherfucker?" Sabretooth growled. "Why do you watch me waste *yours*?" His head started to swing back but before it could, Ann's hand slapped down on it, forcing the gun out of his grip. It clattered across the floor and she immediately jumped after it. So did Sabretooth, but before he could pull the blonde back, Pat shot his leg and he cried out in pain. "BITCH!" he bellowed.

"You know it," Pat replied, blowing on the muzzle of her gun, before re-holstering it. Ann was able to grab the gun and stood, pointing it down at Sabretooth, who was immobilized by the pain in his leg but looked up at the shaky weapon with defiance.

"What are you gonna do, bitch?" he asked. "Shoot me? You don't got the balls."

Ann glared at him but her hands continued to shake. She took a step back and Sabe laughed. Pat shook her head and glanced up at Joe. "You want me to waste him?" she asked.

"No," Joe said, his eyes trained on Ann. "Let her do it." Ann looked up at that and her eyes pleaded with him. She shook her head. "It's alright," he said. "Think about all the horrible things he did to you. Think about what he did to Lourdes, his own girl. He was about to do the same to you. He deserves this, alright? Nobody would blame you for offin' him. And, trust me, it feels so fuckin' good to do an asshole like that in, to give him what he deserves. Just go ahead and you'll see. Trust me, Ann. Do you trust me?" Ann nodded, but continued to waver. "You'll be okay."

She nodded again and pulled the trigger. The sound the gun made was deafening in the silence of the room. Sabretooth's body went limp after the bullet lodged in his cranium and blood splattered over the floor and Ann's bare feet. The gun dropped from her shaky hand to the ground and her knees began to wobble. She looked to Joe for help and he stepped forward, catching her in his arms before she could reach the floor.

"I've got you," he whispered against her hair. "I've got you, Ann." She buried her face into his chest and began to sob as he rubbed her back.

Pat watched with undisguised hurt, but Joe didn't notice. She took a deep breath and swallowed past the lump in her throat, turning to the other men. "Come on," she said, "we don't wanna be around when the fuzz shows up." She stormed past the confused group, not even sparing Joe and Ann a glance over her shoulder to see that he'd lifted the woman into his arms and was now carrying her, bridal-style, out of the room.

Joe's eyes remained focused on Ann the whole time. "I'm gonna get you outta here, okay?" he whispered in her ear. "You'll be okay. Gonna get you somewhere nice and safe, alright?"

"Okay," Ann sniffed against his shirt, her arms tight around his neck already.

It was in that moment that Ann Martin realized how deeply and fathomlessly in love she was with Joe Sullivan.

Chapter Four

It took them less than 24 hours to get Ann cleaned up, patched up, buy her some new clothes, feed her, and purchase her a train ticket to Stamford, CT. Her family lived in Manhattan, but Joe figured it would be too easy for anybody to snatch her here in the city. At least in Connecticut she would be safe with Pat's cousin, Carly.

"Now, listen," he told her once they made it to Grand Central, "Carly's gonna meet you at the platform. Don't be stupid and go wandering off alone, okay? Somebody might come after you and you don't want to be alone when that happens. Carly's tough and protective as all hell; she's the one that's gonna keep you safe in our absence."

"But, Joe, I—" Ann started to argue.

"No," Joe cut her off, shaking his head. "No arguments right now, okay? We're trying to save your life and this is the best way to do it, okay?" Ann nodded, tears in her eyes. "Okay. Now, as soon as we've got everything settled over here, either me or Pat is gonna come get you in Stamford. We'll call Carly first to let you know we're on our way, okay?" Ann nodded and Joe gave her a gentle smile. "You're gonna be okay, kid," he said, cupping her cheek with one hand. "Everything's gonna be okay now." Ann took a deep breath and canted into him, wrapping her arms around his neck and pressing her face into his neck.

"Don't die," she whispered, on a shuddery breath. She pulled back. "Promise me you won't die." Her gaze was steely and Joe couldn't help but nod at that.

"I promise," he said and she smiled sadly up at him, leaning up on her toes to press her lips against his. Joe returned her kiss, his hands cupping her slender hips. Pat watched from the side with a frown, before looking away.

"Better wrap it up," she said, suddenly, looking at her watch. "The train is leaving in about ten minutes." Joe and Ann pulled apart, sighing. Tears streamed down Ann's cheeks and Joe brushed them away with his thumbs.

"Everything will be alright," he said again. "You'll see. Now, go." He backed away from her and Ann took a deep breath, grabbing her bag and heading in the direction of her platform. Before she reached it, she looked back and locked eyes with Joe. She gave him one last wave and blew him a kiss and he offered her a weak smile in return.

When she was gone, Joe's smile disappeared and he turned to Pat. "Let's go get this asshole," he practically growled, starting towards the exit. Pat was right on his heels.

Infiltrating Rick's brownstone was a much harder feet than they'd originally thought. He lived on a more populated street, so the outdoor guards were not an option. That was good in some ways, Joe thought, but now they had no idea exactly how many people were actually *inside* the damn building because every single window was blocked by thick curtains. And in the daytime, there would be no lights on to give even a shadow so they were going in completely blind.

"Listen," Joe said as they planned it all out. "We may lose a few good men today. But I want you all to know how glad I am to have you all on my side. You've remained loyal to me for all these years and I'm grateful for that. Each one of you has a place in my heart."

"Did prison turn you into a sap, Sullivan?" Bardy growled out, making the others laugh. "'Cause I thought it was supposed to make you tougher."

"Looks like it had the opposite effect," TJ piped in, making them all laugh again.

"Fuck you all," Joe laughed, shaking his head. "Alright," he said, "let's get on with it. If anybody finds that bastard before me, keep him alive; I wanna be the one to put that bullet through his skull, got it?" They nodded and broke apart.

Trying to appear inconspicuous, they split into groups, their weapons concealed by clothing and bags. Dove and Pat linked arms like girlfriends and pretended to gossip about their boyfriends, strutting down the street in tight dresses and heels. One group of their men pretended to whistle at them as they passed; another group was dressed as businessmen and carried their weapons in briefcases. Joe had on a hoodie and a pair of headphones in his ears that weren't actually connected to anything. Nobody noticed that they were headed in the exact same direction.

There was an alley in between Rick's brownstone and the one next to it, which they all slipped into, one group at a time. From there, Joe was able to get a good look at the back of the building, through the slats of a broken fence. "There's a fire escape leading into the yard," he told Pat. "We could probably climb it while the others start from the first floor; corner him, ya know?"

Pat nodded. "Good plan," she said. "But there's one leading out the front, too."

"You take one," Joe said, "I'll take the other." It wasn't too complicated.

"What if he's not alone?"

Joe groaned. "TJ, go with Pat; Bardy, come with me." The men nodded. "All the rest, start from the bottom and make your way up. From the looks of it, we've got three floors to deal with here. Make sure Rick gets to the third floor and, remember, don't kill the bastard. I'll handle that part."

There were murmurs of agreement as everybody got into position. Pat and TJ went around the front and climbed up the fire escape, careful not to pass clear in front of a window, lest they give themselves away. Nobody from the street even glanced their way.

Joe and Bardy situated themselves on the back fire escape while the rest of their team waited at every possible entrance for a sign from them to begin.

"Everybody in position?" Joe whispered in his walkie talkie. There was a static of yeses coming from each individual talkie and he took a deep breath. "Okay. Go!" The sound of windows breaking, doors slamming open, shouts and growls and gunfire coming from inside. Joe and Bardy waited for the signal from Dove, telling them that it was safe to enter.

Ann Martin didn't get on the train. She couldn't. Not when she knew that Joe's life was in danger; not when she just recently realized how she felt about him. She just couldn't do it.

So she stood on the platform for fifteen minutes, waved stupidly to the train as it pulled out of the station, and then walked off the platform. She was almost relieved to see that Joe and Pat were no longer standing in the middle of Grand Central when she arrived, surrounded by a thousand other people desperately trying to find their own platforms. Tourists took pictures of the big clock and the constellations painted on the ceilings. They took in everything with wide eyes and even wider mouths, like this train station was something exceedingly special.

Ann had lived here for the whole of her life and she knew that there was absolutely nothing special about this place once you've seen for the hundredth time. Her parents had taken her through here so many times on their way to and from Westchester County, where they had an estate in Purchase, that it wore off by the time she was five. The train station, which had once been a colorful world full of excitement and adventure for a toddler, was now just...loud.

Ann hastened towards the exit as quickly as possible and breathed in the stale New York City air with reverence. She'd almost died just one day before and she never felt so grateful for the chance to breath in the smoky, polluted air of the city, to hear the thundering stutters of construction just down the street. To experience the hateful scowl on a native's face as they bumped into her on the sidewalk. She felt as if she were experiencing New York for the very first time.

Dragging her rolling suitcase behind her, she started in the direction of Washington Square Park. It would take her a while to get there, she knew that, but maybe she could...

Ann paused. What could she do? She didn't have any guns and she knew nothing she could say to Joe would help. He was intent on his revenge, intent on killing another man no matter what the consequences, and she knew that. Knew that he wouldn't stop until he achieved his goal. He would gladly go back to prison if it meant Rick Silas was dead on the ground.

But Ann couldn't let that happen. She couldn't lose him again, not like this. And any other way than Joe killing Rick meant that Rick killed Joe and she couldn't live with that knowledge either. So, no matter how long the distance, or how high the stakes, Ann would have to go after her love. She had to stop him, even if she risked her own life in the process.

He was completely worth it. At least in her mind. She just hoped that she wasn't too late.

"We lost Paulie!" Fisher's voice crackled through the walkie. Joe cursed and shared a look with Bardy, who'd practically been Paulie's guardian since the day he joined, a gangly kid of about 15, desperate to prove himself. Bardy had made him the weapons master he was now. Or had been.

"Sorry, man," Joe whispered. Bardy shook his head, his eyes filled with undisguised rage.

"He's gonna fuckin' pay for that," he growled in a low voice. Joe nodded, solemnly. His walkie crackled again.

"WE'VE GOT HIM!" Mart shouted through the line. "He's headed toward the third floor. Patti! Joey! Do you read me?!"

"Got it!" Pat's voice called and Joe could hear her without the damn talkie. "I'm goin' in!"

"Me too," Joe growled into the machine as he and Bardy readied their guns and stepped up to the window. "

"You ready for this?" Bardy asked in his low, rumbling voice.

Joe nodded. "As I'll ever be," he replied, taking a deep breath. Bardy nodded in return and they both turned to face the window. Joe held up one hand and started a slow countdown on it.

Three....two.....one!

They burst through the window, spilling glass into the room with them. They stumbled slightly at their entrance, but then held their guns up high, pointing them around the room.

It was small and crowded with bedroom furniture; a bed, a chest of drawers, an old vanity table and matching wooden bookcase. The window was next to the door and in the next second a familiar face appeared in the doorway, his hands held up over his head, a smug smile on his face.

"Rick Silas," Joe growled, then spit at the man's feet as they walked past. "Long time, no see."

Rick's head turned in their direction, hands staying up as Pat entered the room after him, her gun pointed at Rick's head. He smirked at the sight of his old foe. "Joseph Sullivan," he greeted. "I thought you were locked up."

"Got out early," Joe replied, his teeth gritted. "Good behavior and all that."

Rick snorted. "Good behavior? You?" He laughed a big, honking laugh. "Right. Ain't nobody gonna get out of jail for 'good behavior' when a senator's daughter gets off; least of all, you." He shook his head. "So how's you get out then?"

"Not really important," Joe replied, his gun still raised. "I'm out now, ain't I? Why dwell on the past?"

"Joey Sullivan," Rick sighed, "always thinking of the future; almost as much as you think of yourself, you greedy bastard."

"At least I'm not some whiny little bitch," Joe said. "So focused on getting my revenge that I put the lives of others at risk."

"That isn't what you're doing right now?" Rick retorted, his eyes skating over the injured men and women behind Joe's back.

"These are all *willing* participants," Joe informed him. "I didn't kill an innocent just to make a point. I'm no pussy when it comes to revenge, Silas. Not like you."

"Nobody's innocent," Rick said, smartly, his hands finally lowering. "You taught me that." He reached for his pocket and they all took a step forward. He put one hand back up. "Relax," he said, pulling out a butane lighter. He flicked it open, then closed. "Nervous habit," he explained, calmly, that smirk never leaving his face. Joe watched him calculatingly, before his eyes began to roam around the room.

For the first time since they burst in, he realized why there had been such opaque curtains hanging in every single window. On every surface, including the floor itself, there were candles; most lit, but some blown out, though wisps of smoke still rose from their wicks as if they'd been lit recently. It was no surprise, really, considering that Rick was a pyromaniac. He always had a lighter handy and enjoyed watching the wax melt on his candles. His weapon of choice was an impromptu flamethrower made from a can of hairspray and whatever lighter he typically had handy at the given moment.

His favorite had a picture of the Tasmanian Devil on it. More than once, Joe had joked that Taz was like the animated incarnation of Rick himself; crazy and unpredictable and incredibly volatile. Rick apparently still favored the character as Joe could just make out the little brown blob on the otherwise silver piece of metal. Some things never changed, he thought, as he continued to glare at the other man.

"I can't believe you still have that damn thing," Joe said, surprising himself even. He hadn't meant to start a conversation.

"My loyalty to Taz hasn't changed," Rick replied, still flicking the lid of his lighter open and close.

"At least you remained loyal to him," Joe retorted on a growl. "At least you remained loyal to *somebody*."

"Still sore about that, are you?" Rick asked, grinning. "I wish you'd just let it go, man. We weren't *that* close."

"I couldn't give a shit less about your little betrayal," Joe informed him. "But what you did *after* that; killing that girl, sending me to prison to *rot* for five fucking years...you had it coming."

"Had what coming?" Rick asked, still smiling as if he didn't know. Joe cocked his gun in response and Rick's grin widened. "Oh," he said. "That." He took a calm breath and shook his head. "You're not *really* going to kill your best chance at going free, are you?" He flicked the lighter open. "The only person who can confirm that you didn't kill that poor Grant girl." He flicked it closed. "Think about it, Joey; if I'm gone, you're just going to go back to prison." Open.

"Not necessarily," Joe countered.

"What else then? You gonna go on the run?" He tilted his head, his eyes shining with amusement. "With your girl, Pat?" Joe's gun wavered and his mouth tightened. "No..." Rick continued with a titter. "That Martin girl? What's her name?" Joe refused to answer but his hand tightened around the gun. "Ann, right?" Joe still did not respond; he didn't have to. "Ann," Rick decided. "How is she? Still smarting from making her first kill?" Joe's eyes widened.

"How did you know about that?" he barked. Rick didn't even blink.

"You still think I don't have eyes everywhere, don't you?" Rick tutted. "Joey, Joey, Joey...when are you gonna learn? I see *everything*," he whispered, his grin becoming catlike.

"See this, punk!" Pat cried as she took a shot. Joe, at the last minute, shoved her arm, causing her bullet to fly at the hand holding Rick's lighter, which dropped on impulse as the man cursed.

"Fucking bitch!" he screamed as he held his hand to his chest. It was bleeding profusely. Joe glared at Pat.

"What did I fucking say?" he growled. She had the decency to look ashamed.

"Sorry," she grumbled. When he turned back to Rick, he was still holding his bleeding hand. And still cursing. "But he deserved it."

"That don't fucking matter," Joe growled at her. "You don't fucking dis—"

"FIRE!" Bardy screamed from behind them. Pat and Joe looked in the direction he was pointing and did, in fact, see a fire begin to bloom from the curtain, where Rick's lit lighter had fallen.

"Shit!" Joe barked, alerting Rick, who turned and let out a string of curses, starting in the direction of the door. Nearly a dozen weapons rose automatically, pointed straight at his head. He paused, turned and ran for the window—the one without the fire escape. He threw aside the curtain and jumped out while everybody watched in shock.

"Did he just fuckin'—" Pat asked.

"Yes," Bardy growled. "Yes, he did."

Joe wasn't convinced. He ran to the window, even as the flames grew around him.

"Joey!" Pat cried. "What the fuck are you doing? We gotta get outta this fuckin' place before it burns to the ground!"

"Go on!" Joe yelled back. "I need to make sure this sonofabitch is dead! I'll take the fire escape."

The others began to run out, some taking the fire escape while other hightailed it down the stairs. "I ain't leavin' you!" Pat cried, even as Dove started to pull her out. Bardy was urging her towards the fire escape, but she wouldn't go.

Joe ignored her, looking out the window. A sadistic grin spread over his features as he spotted Rick's crumpled body in the grass, joints bent at odd angles. He winced once in sympathy and shook his head, backing away from the window.

The room was now engulfed in flames. Those who had rushed to escape had inadvertently knocked over several candles, which only added to the overall fire. The breathable air was diminishing. Pat still stood at the window, hesitant to leave without him. Bardy was tugging on her arm, trying to get her to leave. She refused, pleading with Joe.

He nodded and started after her, before doubling back. He found the lighter next to the lit up curtains and grabbed it: his trophy. He closed it and tucked it deep into his pocket, before turning on his heel and running towards the fire escape.

He'd barely made it with the curtains of those windows burst into flames too, forcing him back. Pat jumped back as well and Bardy attempted to pick her up, but she struggled too much for him to get a good grip.

"We have to go!" he yelled.

"No!" Pat fought. "I won't leave without him!"

"Pat, go!" Joe ordered. "Get out of here!"

"No!" Pat screamed. "Not until I know you're safe!"

"I've got a plan," Joe called back, before turning and running straight to the other window. He took a deep breath before he took a flying leap straight out of it.

"JOE!" Pat screamed just as Bardy got a good hold of her and carried her down the steps.

Joe had jumped out of windows before, but never on the third floor—not when there wasn't a pool below or something else to break his fall. He'd read somewhere that you could lessen the impact by rolling in midair. Well, whoever said that was apparently an idiot who'd never jumped out of a window in their life.

He rolled as soon as he felt himself fly the air—a front flip that would make any amateur gymnast proud—but it did nothing to numb the impact of the ground as he hit it. If anything, it made the fall worse, more painful. Joe could hear the sickening sound of the bones in his legs cracking as he reached the ground. His spine tingled as if pins and needles were stuck all along it, and the pain as his head connected with the ground was like nothing he'd ever felt before. He saw stars appear in front of his eyes. The entire world went silent for a long moment and he thought he died.

He closed his eyes, welcoming it. He'd done what he'd come here to accomplish. The result was lying about a foot away, in worse shape than him, no doubt. He attempted to turn his head but everything hurt and even with his eyes closed he felt his world spinning on its access. So he just lay there, waiting for death to claim him.

As he waited, a ringing started in his ears, muffled crying rising over it. He started to slowly come back to the world, his eyes creaking open, the world blurried until he blinked a couple times and then…

"Ann?" Joe croaked. "Ann, what—?"

"No," Ann whimpered, placing a finger over his lips. "Don't speak, Joe. You're going to be alright, okay? There's an ambulance on the way; they said not to move you." Joe tried to not but that caused even more pain so he settled for breathing. Ann sniffled. "Oh Joe," she sighed. "Joe, you can't leave me. Not now. I need you, baby. You need to hold out; just a little longer."

"Can't," Joe croaked. "Dying."

"No!" Ann cried. "No, you're not; don't say that."

"But, I-I am," he replied. "And th-that's okay."

"No, it's not!" Ann sobbed. "Don't say that! Please don't say that!" Joe shut his eyes and took a breath. When he opened them again, Pat was there. He turned to look at her.

"Pat," he sighed. "Take...take care of her for me, will ya?"

"Don't talk like that, Joey," Pat sniffled. "You're gonna be just fine, alright? Just fine."

"No," Joe sighed. "I'm not. And if...when I'm not here to protect her...you've gotta...okay? Promise me."

"Joe, I—"

"*Promise*," Joe growled.

Pat took a shuddering breath. "Okay," she said. "I promise."

"Good," Joe breathed, turning his eyes back to Ann.

"She'll take good care of you, okay?" he said. Ann nodded, tearfully.

"So will you," she insisted. "You promised. You promised everything would be alright."

Joe sighed. "I'm sorry," he said. "I don't think I'm...I'm going to be able to..." he trailed off and took another breath. "I'm sorry," he said, closing his eyes. After a long, tense moment, they opened again. "Ann," he breathed. "I...I have to tell you something."

"What?" Ann asked, leaning down again. His voice was becoming faint.

"I...I loved you," Joe breathed out, before his eyes shut permanently and his body went completely limp.

Both Pat and Ann dissolved into tears, the former holding the latter as Ann held on to Joe's body, their tears mingling as they fell to his chest. Above their wails, ambulance sirens could be heard.

THE END

TWO KILLERS & A HOOKER

JAKE MICHAELS

CHAPTER ONE

Jesse James Hewitt never knew when the killings would come.

All he knew was that violence was the only tool he had.

He wasn't like other serial killers who stalked their victims and preplanned their attacks. Jesse's victims were random, in all shapes, sizes and colors.

That is how he stayed under the radar.

But his hair trigger temper could go off at any time. Right now, as he parked the stolen Toyota Camry in front of the corner grocery store, he felt happy. He had a little money in his pocket and for the next week had a place to stay at his uncle's pad.

Jesse James did, in fact, look like a modern Jesse James. He wore flared out jeans with a leather vest over a blue denim shirt. He ditched the skin head look years ago and instead grew his hair out long, a tousled mop of brown curls that he rarely combed. He had ice blue eyes that charmed many a woman until they got to know the man behind the eyes and soon felt repulsed.

Jesse walked into the store and noticed the young Asian kid leafing through the latest X-men in front of the comic rack.

He approached the young man, startling him as he craned his neck to look at his comic book cover.

"Wolverine and Kitty Pryde!" Jesse said. "Yeah, I'd fuck her."

Walking through the store, Jesse whistled in tune with the Taylor Swift swing that played on the overhead radio. Bored, he picked up a loaf of Wonderbread off the shelf then tossed it aside. Heading toward the beverage aisle, he reached inside the glass and picked up a bottle of his favorite drink.

Chocolate Yoo-Hoo.

He ripped off the lid and guzzled the contents down, the chocolate milk dripping off the side of his mouth.

Belching loud, he drifted over to the second of the three store aisles, grabbing a box of chocolate donuts. His thick fingers ripped through the plastic, breaking off a piece of a donut.

Jesse looked out at the store front window as a police car sped down the street, sirens blaring. Another squad car followed, then another.

"Uh oh," Jesse cried out. "The natives are restless."

Jesse tossed a chunk of the chocolate donut into his mouth before placing the box on the cashier's counter. An Ethiopian girl, no more than twenty years old, gave him a courtesy smile which quickly disappeared. She had caramel-colored skin and had dyed her hair blonde, leaving the tips dark brown. Her name tag read 'Naomi'.

"Hi," Jesse said.

"You find everything okay?" she asked.

"Definitely," he said, eyeballing the slim young woman up and down. "Anybody ever tell you that you look like Jessica Alba?"

"Who?"

"You know, the actress. Full lips. Beautiful face. If she were black, you'd look just like her. Or maybe she'd look just like you."

"I don't know who you're talking about," Naomi said.

"That's charming," he said. "Where are you from?"

"Ethiopia."

"I would have guessed Eritrea," he said, guzzling down the Yoo-Hoo.

"I need to scan it," she said, holding her hand out.

"Oh right," he said, handing the bottle to the young woman.

"Do you like your job?"

"Will this be all, sir?" Naomi asked, ignoring his question.

"No," Jesse said. "You're a beautiful girl and I'm really interested in how you got here and where you're going. What time do you get off?"

"When do I get off?"

"As often as you can, right?" Jesse laughed loud.

Naomi rolled her eyes.

He looked back at the storefront window. "Open twenty-four seven. How about you? Are you open twenty-four seven?"

"Is this your best game?"

"You couldn't handle my game with a referee and a whistle."

Naomi punched buttons on the cash register. "That will be five dollars."

"Think about it," he said. "You. Me. A glass of scotch in front of a warm fire."

"I don't think so."

"Can you look me in the eye when you say that?"

Naomi complied with his request, her facial expression annoyed. "I'll say this real slow so that you can understand. I. Don't. Think. So."

"I have to take you out," Jesse said. "Sometimes, you meet a person and you just know, do you know what I mean, baby?"

"Five dollars, asshole."

"Asshole," Jesse said, his eyes flickering from lust to hatred. "Is that what I am?"

"Sometimes you meet a person and you just know, do you know what I mean?"

"I just hate it," Jesse said, pulling out his gun. "When people come to this country."

He fired into the girl's stomach.

"And they don't see that I'm a local boy that made good."

Jesse grabbed his box of donuts and headed out of the store, leaving Naomi writhing in pain on the floor. The Asian boy dropped the comic and cowered in fear.

Jesse sneered at the young man then feinted as if he were about to shoot him.

"Boo!"

The Asian kid bolted out of the store, running across the street and into traffic. Horns blared.

"Run!" Jesse laughed, blowing the coils of smoke away from his gun. "Run, China Boy, Run!"

CHAPTER TWO

Kelly had walked up and down the liquor aisle for over a half-hour now. Usually, there would be someone in his face asking if he needed help. But this storekeeper seemed content to watch the television up on the corner wall. An obese woman with tinted eyeglasses she stared up at the television screen oblivious to her surroundings.

Kelly knew the feeling. He felt like everything around him was television and that he was an uncredited player in the script. His emotions felt as if they were trapped in quicksand, his tumultuous childhood traumatizing his brain into an endless loop of bad memories.

A permanent nightmare.

Kelly thought he looked inconspicuous. He wore a Golden State Warriors baseball cap and a long black trench coat two sizes too big. Wire-rimmed glasses covered his face which he always kept downcast, giving him the look of a schoolyard pervert. Underweight and undersized, Kelly cultivated the creepy look. It kept people away from him.

"I can't do it," he muttered. "I can't fucking do it."

He went up and down the aisle again but this time he grabbed the bottle of 'two buck Chuck' and hid it inside his trench coat.

"You can do it," he hissed. "Just fucking do it."

He turned down the aisle again.

"No, I can't," Kelly placed the bottle back on the shelf.

"What the fuck are you doing?" Jesse asked, blocking the path of the young man.

"Excuse me?"

"You don't want the booze?"

"No, sir."

"What's wrong with it."

"I'm trying to give it up."

"Everybody's trying to give something up," Jesse said, taking the bottle of Two Buck Chuck back off the shelf. "That's why everybody is so damn miserable. You gotta do the things you love!"

Kelly looked over at the cashier who sat oblivious to their conversation. He saw that her name tag read 'Rosie'.

"See this?" Jesse asked, holding up the bottle of Chocolate Yoo-hoo. "My dentist says I have to stop drinking these. Causes a bunch of cavities. And heart disease. But I can't stop myself. Tastes too damn good. Want to try?"

Kelly shook his head.

Jesse took another swig of his chocolate then eyeballed the wine bottle. "2014. Vintage! You like the old stuff?"

"Yes, sir."

Jesse popped open the cork. "Here," he said, extending the bottle to Kelly. "Try it."

Kelly looked away, a nervous tic in his neck.

"What's wrong? Cat got your tongue?"

"No, sir."

"You got issues," Jesse said, watching Kelly twitch as he started to back down the aisle.

"What's wrong now?" Jesse asked.

Kelly backed into a Mexican woman with a cart full of six packs. She looked to be nine months pregnant.

"Damn, *mamacita*," Jesse said as the woman walked by. "Way to start the kid off right."

"*Chinga tu madre*," the woman said.

"*Adios, amiga*," Jesse rolled his eyes, walking toward Kelly. "You see, that is what I'm talking about. Poor kid has a mother that is boozing it up and he isn't even out of the womb yet. He's got no chance, that kid. Starting off life behind the eight-ball with a mother like that, right?"

Kelly nodded his head in agreement.

"Come on," Jesse said, motioning Kelly to follow him. "You're a cool dude. Good listener. Sometimes you look at somebody and you just know, you know what I mean?"

The two stepped over to the cashier who never took her eye off the television. A game of Jeopardy was on.

Jesse handed the woman a $20 bill for the $15 bottle.

"Here you are, ma'am," he said. "Keep the change."

The cashier rolled her eyes.

"I think you and I are on the same frequency," Jesse said, leading Kelly out of the store. "Are you from the Bay Area?"

"No sir," Kelly said.

"Well, we don't have that in common. But that's okay."

He handed the bottle of wine to Kelly. "Are there houses of ill-repute where you're from?"

"What's that?"

"No worries, buddy, no worries," Jesse said. "I'm going to show you the time of your damn life. Gonna be like two sailors out on leave. That's right. That's just what we're going to do."

The cashier turned her head away from the television as a news report came on.

The reporter talked about a serial killer on the loose. White male, black baseball cap and glasses.

Rosie paid no mind to the broadcast, she walked to the front door and flipped over the closed sign.

The West Oakland sky had darkened, leaving blood orange hues of pollution on the horizon.

"Look at this shit," Jesse said as they walked down the street outside the liquor store. He shook his head as he gazed upon the abandoned storefronts and houses covered in graffiti. "Street art, my ass. Bunch of crap. Broken windows. Broken condoms. Broken lives. The fuck is wrong with these people?"

Kelly looked unnerved as the light in front of them turned red.

"Come on," Jesse said, crossing against the light. "What are you a Boy Scout?"

Kelly squinted as he looked up at the red light.

"Let's go, dude."

The light turned green and he continued to follow Jesse, not knowing why.

"Where you parked?" Jesse asked.

"I don't have a car."

"You walked? This is a dangerous place for a white boy. I mean we can walk down the streets here in Oakland and nothing will happen to us. Maybe. But absence of evidence isn't evidence of absence. We walk around here long enough someone will try and rob us. That's why we have to stick together. Can't be walking around alone, just one white boy against ten of them-"

"I take the bus," Kelly said. "I have a disability."

"Disability? What kind?"

"Mental."

"Like, you see psychiatrists and shit?"

"Yes, sir."

"Are you crazy?"

"No, sir. I just see and dream about things. And I do things. Sometimes I can't remember if it was real or a dream."

"But you do see a psychiatrist?"

"Yes, sir."

"They worth the money?"

"County pays for it. Plus I get a free bus pass."

"Right on," Jesse said. "Hey, if everyone else in this city gets freebies so can we. People around here are so ugly they make my eyes hurt. They can give them all the welfare they want as long as I don't have to see them. Man, if I were president I would change things, that's for shit-sure. I would test out bio-weapons here. You know, chemicals and shit. Release it into the atmosphere, turn these assholes into mutants. Kinda like the Island of Dr. Moreau. It would be awesome."

"Yes, sir."

"Well, will you look at that."

The two stop in front of a parked Mercedes. Jesse pointed at the bumper sticker that read "Co-Exist" and "Peace."

"See that's what I'm talking about," Jesse said. "Can you believe this shit? Perfectly good German car and they put all that shit on there. Co-exist? Muslims are taking over our damn country and we got assholes with bumper stickers promoting-"

Working himself into a fury, Jesse kicked in the rear brake light before finishing his sentence.

The car alarm went off and startled Kelly.

"Teee haaaawww!" Jesse said, smashing in the other brake light. "Come on!"

Kelly followed Jesse as they ran over to a dilapidated Toyota Camry across the street. The license plate read BAD AZZ.

"This is me," Jesse said, walking to the passenger side door and unlocking it. "Saw the license plate and just had to have it."

"I can't go with you, sir."

"Why not? I think you're cool."

"I don't know you, sir."

"I ain't a fag. Do you think I'm a fag?"

"No, sir."

"Well, let's do this," Jesse reached into his back holster and took out his gun, taking the clip out and then shoving it back in. "Now get in the fuckin' car and let's get rowdy like good sailors should."

Kelly nodded and got into the vehicle.

"Nice to see you changed your mind," Jesse said, hiding the gun in his back pocket again. "Only fools and the dead never changed their mind."

CHAPTER THREE

Jesse drove down the street like a maniac, alternately speeding up then slowing down. He swerved in front of cars, flipping the bird indiscriminately.

Kelly stared straight ahead looking scared shitless.

"Look man, I didn't mean to pull the gun on you," Jesse said. "I promised you a good time, right? We gonna get some whores. Show you what a cool guy I am. How's that sound?"

Kelly shrugged his shoulders.

"The Warriors ain't playing tonight," Jesse pointed at Kelly's baseball cap. "You watch the game last night?"

"No."

"Me neither," Jesse said. "Shit, why do that when you can go out and get some poontang, you know what I mean?"

Jesse looked out the side window and saw a blonde woman walking down the street. Dressed in business attire, her suit did little to conceal her figure.

"Holy shit!" Jesse slowed the vehicle down. "Curves for days!"

The woman turned her head and looked at the men staring at her.

"Hey darlin'" Jesse said.

Rolling her eyes, the woman turned around and began walking in the opposite direction.

"Well, fuck you then," Jesse laughed. "We could have you cumming instead of going, ain't that right, friend?"

Looking up ahead, Jesse saw a brunette walking, her eyes focused on her cell phone.

"Hot, hot, hot," Jesse said. "All these young Cal students out here sometimes. Usually trying to score some dope. What is your type? Me? I don't really have a type. I like them all really. Tall, short. Big ass. Little ass. I just like pulling girls hair. That's what gets me off. It's primal, you know. Doggy style."

They slow down and see a prostitute up ahead. She's blonde, very tall and leaning up against the pole of a bus stop.

Upon seeing Jesse's car slowing down, she twirled around the pole, like a stripper.

"Here we go," Jesse lowered his voice. "Think we might have a live one here."

Jesse stopped the vehicle next to the woman who poked her head in on the passenger side.

"Hey boys, you need a date?"

Her face had pock-marks, as if she had small-pox. Her half-lidded jaundice eyes a dead giveaway of her crack whore status.

Jesse slammed on the gas. "Good God! Did you see that? I've seen ugly but goddamn! And she had no teeth! Then again she doesn't need teeth for what she does!"

Jesse looked over at Kelly and noticed him staring at a different brunette up ahead. The girl stood with her arms crossed, emphasizing her ample cleavage.

"There you go," Jesse said. "There you go."

He stopped the car in front of the woman.

Upon closer inspection, her hair was dark blonde with brown streaks. A light skinned Latina, with full lips and green eyes. In her mid-twenties, she smiled wide as Jesse drove up.

"Two good looking guys in here. How's it going?"

"Will you do the things she won't?" Jesse asked.

"I'm the girl your mami and your papi warned you about," she said. Her voice breathy, with an accented lilt, like a breeze combing through dry leaves on a hot summer night.

"What's good on the menu?"

"That depends on how hungry you boys are," the woman said, reaching down and grabbing Kelly's crotch on 'hungry.'

Kelly shuddered in fear.

"My friend over here is starving," Jesse laughed. "As in he has not had a meal in years, if you catch my drift."

"Well, there will be plenty on the plate for both of you."

"Hop in, *mamacita*," Jesse said.

Kelly watched as the woman got into the car. His heart began to pound and his throat began to feel parched, her sweet perfume quickly filling the vehicle.

Reminding him of his mother.

CHAPTER FOUR

"My name is Maricela," she said from the backseat, looking over at Kelly on the passenger side.

Kelly said nothing, holding the wine bottle to his chest and pursing his lips.

"Is he mute?" Maricela asked Jesse. "Or deaf?"

"He doesn't open up until he really trusts someone," Jesse said. "He's smart that way. Do you always judge people?"

"I'm not judging," Maricela said. "Just asked him a damn question."

"Now you're trying to make him feel bad," Jesse said. "You're supposed to make us feel good. Make me and him feel like kings. Right, Kelly?"

Jesse reached over and playfully hit Kelly in the arm.

"I'll do that and more," Maricela said.

"Damn skippy," Jesse said. "Tee haaawww!"

"You're not high are you?" she asked.

"I'm high on life," Jesse said. "Hangin' with my homie here and about to bust a nut on a fine ass Latina."

"Well, thank you, handsome."

"Here," Jesse reached over and took the wine bottle out of Kelly's hand. "Let's get this party started."

Kelly grabbed the wine back, agitated.

"I didn't mean what I said," Maricela said to Kelly, running her fingers through the hair underneath his cap. "You seem nice. And cute. Sometimes you just know, you know what I mean? You look at someone and you get a feeling about them. It is a survival trait among us escorts."

Kelly pulled back then gave in to the woman's touch.

"There you go," Jesse said. "My friend here is an introvert. Just takes some time before he opens up to you."

"I've seen it all, dude, believe me," Maricela said. "There was this guy the other night who wanted me to shave off his chest hair. And there was this other dude that wanted me to take out this dildo he had shoved up his ass. When I took it out, the dildo was still vibrating."

"Sick fucker," Jesse said. "What a sick fuck."

"Can you imagine shoving a dildo up your ass and than calling an escort to fish it out?" Maricela asked.

"My imagination can't go that far," Jesse said.

"Maybe he called one escort to put it in and then called another to take it out?" Kelly asked.

"There you go," Jesse said. "See? He needs to get to know you before he talks."

"There's my place," Kelly said, pointing in the distance.

The television was already on when the trio stepped inside. A news reporter held up a bottle of Charles Shaw wine, explaining how forensics determined the amount of poison that a serial killer used to murder his victims.

"Nice!" Jesse said as he entered Kelly's house. Faded flowered prints marked the wallpaper but Kelly had no pictures or paintings, only one mirror in the center of the living room.

Maricela walked over to the mirror, dabbing her make-up and adjusting her cleavage.

"This is a nice place, friend," Jesse said. "I can spend lots of time up in here. We can watch TV, play video games, shoot the shit. Do you have an X-Box? My kind of place here."

Kelly said nothing as he entered the kitchen and set the wine bottle down, half-listening as Jesse continued to jabber on.

On the counter, he saw the rat poison and weed killer boxes next to the wine bottle. He quickly grasped the incriminating evidence and shoved them into his trench coat.

"Not a bad view," Jesse said, opening than closing the window curtain. "This place is what blue collar is supposed to look like. Nothing fancy. Just warm coziness. This is America! Shit man, we should go out and get an apple pie to go with that wine."

"You sound like a politician," Maricela said.

"I am the King," Jesse said. "A king. Have you ever been to L.A.?

"Yeah, I go down south sometimes."

"I was there last month. Hollywood. What a bunch of freaks! I went there thinking I could get away from all these Occupy Idiots and what happens? I get caught up in their protest! Wanted to shoot every one of those tree-hugging bitches!"

Kelly placed the poison inside a cabinet and tried to step back out of the kitchen when Jesse stepped in front of him.

"Freakin' idiots!" Jesse screamed in Kelly's face. "Do you know what I mean? These fuckers should go out and get a damn job. Am I right?"

"Right," Kelly nodded his head.

"That's right, buddy," Jesse said, sidestepping Kelly and entering the kitchen. "What kind of grub you got, man?"

Jesse ignored the ant trail on the counter and opened the refrigerator. "What kind of goodies do we have going on in here?"

Kelly crossed and uncrossed his arms, looking nervous.

"Nice!" Jesse said. "Hey man, there is only one ice cream flavor in the world. Only one. Care to guess?"

Kelly shook his head.

Jesse took out an ice cream carton from the freezer in triumph. "Vanilla! Damn, we have a lot in common."

Jesse opened up one of the drawers and grabbed a spoon.

"Come on," Jesse said. "Let's get the party started."

The two walked back into the living room.

Maricela has her shirt off, standing there wearing nothing but a black bra and jeans.

"Wow," Jesse said.

"You like?"

"Nice artwork," Jesse's eyes scanned up and down Maricela's tattooed body. A snake went down her left arm and she had pentagrams on both shoulders. "You're a devil woman."

"I got into the occult in college," Maricela said, looking down at her own tattoos. "Did a mid-term paper on this occult in Mexico then I got interested in the stuff. This one here is the eye of horus."

Maricela pointed down at her belly-button, the Egyptian symbol of protection inked on her stomach.

"So gentleman," she said. "Are we going one at a time or is this a threesome?"

"My friend here goes first," Jesse said, scooping out a spoonful of the ice cream and letting holding it out to Maricela. "Let's make it special."

Mariccla wrapped her lips around the spoon, sucking off the ice cream as she sat down on the chair behind her.

"No," Kelly squealed.

Maricela sprang out of the seat.

"Not that chair!" he yelled.

Maricela stepped away from the chair and gave Jesse a startled look. "Are you sure he's alright?"

"I said don't judge him," Jesse said before taking a few steps back with the young man. "You hearing voices?"

"Loud and clear," Kelly said.

"Alright now," Jesse said. "That's nothing to be ashamed of. You should be proud of that. Been hearing voices all your life and you're still here. You're a damn soldier."

"I am?"

"Hell fucking yeah," Jesse said. "But she'll help you get rid of those voices, okay?"

Jesse patted Kelly on the back before heading into the kitchen.

"Relax, dude," Maricela whispered.

Kelly slowly turned his back to the young woman but she spun him around gently.

"It is really easy," Maricela said, taking Kelly by the hand. "First timers are my specialty."

She lead him to the chair to sit down and he shuddered.

"Easy," Maricela said. "We don't have to do it there."

She placed her hands on both of his shoulders and led him over to the couch.

Kelly sat down, eyes downcast.

Maricela played with unbuckling his belt until he turned away.

"Okay, okay, we can do other things."

She let the strap of her bra fall down off her shoulder.

Kelly looked up with painful shyness, licking his cracked lips as he stared at Maricela's breasts.

"You're a titty man," she laughed. "There you go."

Maricela took his hand and placed it on her left breast, letting the young man knead away.

"Gently," she said, tilting her head back in pleasure. "Gently. There you go. You like that?"

Kelly nodded, noticing the upside down cross that Maricela had tattooed on the underside of her wrist.

"Me too, baby. Me too."

Kelly turned to the kitchen door and shuddered as he saw Jesse standing there, watching.

"What are you doing?" Jesse asked. "I said he is a beginner. He's shy with women. You gotta take it slow."

"You get off on taking a front row seat?" Maricela asked. "We were taking it slow."

"Then why is he so freaked out?"

Maricela glared at Jesse.

"Come on," Jesse said, waving her away from the couch. "Give us a minute here. Go upstairs to the bedroom and we'll be right there. We need to have a man to man."

Maricela got up off the couch, rolling her eyes as she made her way up the steps.

"This always works for me," Jesse said, waving the wine bottle in his hand as he sat down next to Kelly. "Loosens you up. Breaks down whatever blockages you got going on in your big head and little head."

Kelly gulped hard.

"We'll be right there!" Jesse called out. "Go ahead and get nekkid! He'll be right up."

CHAPTER FIVE

Maricela entered the bedroom and closed the door. The lamp on the desk illuminated the neatly made bed. There were pictures of dead bugs on the wall which gave her the creeps. She looked closer and realized that they weren't pictures at all. They were dead moths and butterflies inserted between the glass and cardboard backing.

A buck is a buck, she thought, seeing more than her share of strange. She walked over to the TV set and pushed the button to turn it on, looking for the remote control on the counter.

"Look man," Jesse said, putting his arm around Kelly like a big brother. "There is only one thing you need to know about women, okay? You have to satisfy their needs. Once you do that, you are in. Okay? So do you know what women want more than anything?"

"Help?"

"No, they want to get high," Jesse said, removing his arm around Kelly, struggling to uncork the wine bottle he held between his legs. "You just have to find out what women want. Some women you meet are going to want fun. Power. Status. Money. That is why whores like

Maricela are so great. There is no drama. You pay your fee and get what you want."

Jesse popped the cork on the bottle and Kelly shuddered. He knew he had placed the poison in that one.

Jesse raised the bottle to his lips but Kelly grabbed it out of his hands.

"No!"

Jesse stared at Kelly for a beat.

"You never got to have any fun did you?" Jesse asked.

"She used to send me to the store," Kelly said. "With a note to get booze."

"Your mom?"

Kelly nodded.

"No worries, man," Jesse said, moving closer to Kelly now. "My folks were the same way. Both of them alcoholics. Dad was a functional one. Went to work every day. Worked his ass off every day. Then one day he shot himself. Just stepped into the house and blew his brains out. Died all alone."

"I never knew my Dad. Never. No pictures. Nothing. Bet he died alone."

"My mom didn't even cry," Jesse said. "Just kept bringing men over. Fucked every one. Didn't care if I was listening or watching or what. Definitely didn't care that my Dad found out. She was evil, man. Evil incarnate."

"Mine too," Kelly whispered, hunching his back as of the ghost of his mother could hear him.

"Mine was worse than an evil step mom. She was a real mom."

Maricela laid on the bed, noodling around on her cell phone which now showed a dead battery. Looking around for an extension so she could recharge it, the screen shot on the television caught her eye.

The report showed a police sketch of a man that resembled Jesse.

"Police said to be on the lookout for the license plate BAD AZZ in a late model white or gray Toyota. If you have any information regarding the suspect please call 911 immediately."

Maricela toggled on her cell phone again. Dead.

She ran over to the bedroom door but when he opened it she saw Jesse standing outside with Kelly behind him.

"Someone is in a hurry to get started," Jesse said. "If you're that horny you can go ahead and start without us."

"Was just wondering where you guys were," she said.

"He's ready and rarin' to go," Jesse said, placing his arm around Kelly and shaking him. "Go get 'em, Tiger."

Maricela forced a smile, stepping aside to let the men in.

"You ready to show him a good time?" Jesse asked.

"But of course," she said, her voice quavered, betraying her nervousness. "Give the man a little privacy."

Maricela took Kelly by the hand and led him further into the bedroom. She attempted to close the door but Jesse stopped her.

"Nothing goes on behind closed doors around here," Jesse said.

Kelly looked back at Jesse as if he were about to go into the electric chair.

"You can do it, buddy!"

"Come on, handsome," Maricela motioned for Kelly to sit down on the bed. The young man took a deep breath, eyes downcast until he slowly looked up at woman stroking his upper thigh. "Do you think I'm pretty?" she asked.

Kelly could only nod his head, smitten by her beauty.

"Thanks," she said.

Jesse made as if he were going down the steps but stopped at the top, kneeling down so he remained out of Maricela's eyeline.

He listened to Maricela's voice, his heart beating in anticipation of what came next just like when his mother had men over at the house.

"You look like a movie star," Kelly blurted out. "Like you should be in porn or something."

"We should go someplace else," Maricela said. "Just the two of us. Okay?"

"But what about my friend? You don't like him?"

"I like you better," she said, kissing him on the lips then hugging him.

Kelly shuddered in delight.

"You have to leave," she said, nuzzling his ear. "This dude is a serial killer. Okay? He'll kill us both."

"What the hell is going on here?" Jesse asked stepping through the door, his entire body an antennae telling him that something was up.

"This young stud is pitching up a tent!" Maricela said, standing back up and pointing at Kelly's crotch.

Jesse grabbed her wrist before she could walk back downstairs. "Where are you going?"

"I have to get us some protection. Duh." Maricela hurried out of the bedroom.

Jesse sat down next to Kelly. "What did she say to you?"

"She has a crush on me."

"Ha!" Jesse laughed. "See? See what happens when you give women what they want. You gonna start listening to me now?"

They both hear Maricela's high heels running down the steps.

Jesse sprinted down the stairs and caught her just as she reached the door.

He spun her around, angry. "It ain't polite to leave a party early! Thought you were going to get some protection?"

"I left the rubbers in the car."

"Left the rubbers in the car, bullshit!" Jesse slammed her against the wall. "You're a damn devil. A thief!"

Jesse reached inside Maricela's purse and pulled out a wallet.

Kelly's wallet.

"Stop!" Kelly said, coming down the steps.

"Lifted it straight outta your pocket, dude!" Jesse threw the wallet back at Kelly.

Maricella ran over to the wine bottle on the coffee table and smashed it against the edge. Grasping the bottle by the handle, she held it in front of her as a weapon.

"Ooooh," Jesse said. "Come on, bitch! Come on, let's see what you got!"

Maricela's face contorted into that of feral woman, fighting for her life. She stabbed at Jesse, lacerating his hand with the glass.

"Bitch!" he said.

Maricela ran toward the kitchen.

Jesse gave chase until Kelly jumped on his back.

"Leave her alone!" Kelly screamed.

Jesse threw off the little man with ease, pushing him into the chair. "You crazy? This bitch just tried to rob you, man!"

Racing through the kitchen, Maricela opened the cellar door and locked it behind herself.

"Bitch!" Jesse screamed, pounding on the wood. "Bitch!"

He kicked the cellar door again and again.

"Fuck off!" Maricela cried out.

Jesse looked down at his hand, his blood dripping on the kitchen floor.

Walking back into the living room, he saw Kelly sitting on the couch watching TV, another wine bottle in his hand.

"Dude!" Jesse said, holding up his bloodied hand. "Look what your damn girlfriend did to me."

"She's not my girlfriend."

"Where's the key to your basement?" Jesse asked, taking out his gun. "Or do I have to just blow shit open?"

"I have the key," Kelly said, glaring at Jesse.

"Hey man," Jesse said. "You're looking at me with some hate in your eye. I told you that girl was a thief. A demon. You see that upside cross on her wrist? She's a devil worshiper! Doesn't Satanism freak you the fuck out? Let's go kill her ass."

"She's already dead," Kelly said, staring off into the distance, in his own world.

"All of mine are dead too," Jesse said pointing the gun at his own temple. "So let's kill another one."

"She told me she loved me."

"Of course," Jesse said. "I knew that. That's why I got her for you. Figured she was just your type."

He took the wine bottle out of Kelly's hand and guzzled it down. "Aaaaahhh!"

Kelly returned his attention to the television, his eyes transfixed.

"What is it, goddamnit?" Jesse asked, turning toward the TV. He saw the police sketch of himself and the license plate.

BAD AZZ.

Enraged, he shot a bullet through the TV.

CHAPTER SIX

Maricela heard the gunshot. Startled, she looked around the cellar for a weapon of any kind. She found a fire poker in the corner and gripped it hard.

Kelly ran back toward the cellar door with the keys in hand. "I'll get you out," he called out to Maricela. "I'll help you."

Jesse chased after him but fell down, the room spinning, his entire body sweating. He retched again, with blood streaked bile coming out of his mouth. He looked at Kelly staring at him, wild-eyed with fear. His friend went in and out of focus, doubling and distorting like a kaleidoscope.

What was in that wine?

Maricela took the fire poker and smashed out the tiny cellar windows.

"Help me!" she screamed. "I've been kidnapped! Help me!"

Kelly put the key in the cellar lock but could not get it to open.

Jesse pitched forward over the sink and retched again.

"The fuck you put into that wine?" Jesse asked, purple bile spilling out of his mouth.

"I'm sorry," Kelly said.

Falling to the ground, Jesse pointed the gun at Kelly.

"I was just trying to be a good friend," Jesse said.

Maricela screamed as she heard the gunshot.

She scrambled back up the cellar steps. Pressing her ear to the door, she waited several minutes before she unlocked it.

Opening up the door, she saw both Jesse and Kelly on the floor in a growing pool of blood.

Kelly laid on his stomach, the blood spewing forth from the fatal gunshot blast into his belly. He stared straight ahead at Jesse who laid on his back, blood and foam caked around his lips, neck and chest.

Ants began to scuttle over their bodies.

They were both locked in a death stare at each other. The pupils of their eyes like black holes eating the whites.

Their once lonely faces no longer dark but relieved.

They didn't have to die alone.

KISS THE SUN

JESSICA OLSEN

The heist had been planned for months, almost a year. Julian was the ringleader, but all of them had been thinking of it for while.

Rock lost his job during the last series of factory shutdowns. His parents had been of the mentality that there would always been work in manual labor and had never been particularly bothered by his poor grades. He had trusted them and his trust had backfired. As the years went by, work in his field of expertise dried up. He retrained again and again, moving from factory to factory as he was repeatedly replaced by machines. His work was reduced to minimum wage jobs in warehouses. He had considered moving to the country and working on a farm, but jobs there were drying up too. He was terrified of leaving the home he knew and the people he liked to spend the rest of his life picking strawberries on a by the pound salary. When Julian had suggested the heist, Rock was in. He had considered turning to crime before, but had never known anyone to cooperate with and didn't really feel he had the intellect to pull it off. Julian on the other hand, overshadowed Rock in intelligence, background knowledge and the contacts they needed. Rock trusted Julian implicitly. And at that stage, he didn't really have a choice any more.

Electra had been roped into it less willingly than Rock could have suspected. She and Julian had been together for two years when he came up with the plan, but she felt it may be time to move on. Julian was intelligent, talented and educated. He was also amazingly good looking. She had been drawn in by his gorgeous dark locks and green eyes and she had stayed in hopes that his talent would eventually lead to a big-time breakthrough. After the first year, her hopes had begun to fade. She had found Julian to be lazy and arrogant. She had also found him to be very good at spending all his money on alcohol and strip clubs. Over the second year she had drifted away. Coming to terms with her plumpening figure and the first grays on her head, she had started looking elsewhere, wondering what her life would have been like if she'd chosen better. When Julian had first proposed the plan she had laughed in his face, packed a small bag and spent the night at her best friend's house. But he patiently waited until she had thought it through and, as she considered it, the prospect of her cut, a cool four hundred thousand, was inviting. She wasn't sure whether she'd stay with him afterward, but she was happy to string along for another few months if there was a chance she could get all that. It was better than going back to selling weed anyway.

Harry Julian was the mastermind. As Electra had found out, despite his intellect, talent and several hundred thousand dollars worth of business school, he wasn't particularly interested in hard graft. He came up with numerous plans and get rich quick schemes. He bought and sold flats, invested in shares, started a nation wide weed business and turned his hand to running a bailiff company. Many of them were successful. But after they succeeded he would drain the funds and go on holiday where he would get drunk and visit strip clubs until the money was all gone and he was back at step one. When nothing was left he wanted to do something new. Only this time he felt he had an edge. He had spent many years of internship working at a bank that was currently being remodeled. They had decided to stay open during the refurbishment, leaving several key spots vulnerable. The amount of money the bank held would be less, but still enough for almost one and a half million to be almost within Julian's grasp. This would be the pot of gold he would retire on. Of course, he had to find trustworthy people to help him. He approached a few old business associates, but only one of them, Rock, a mild-mannered, high school dropout of a thug, was happy to go through with it. He wasn't bright enough to help with the planning, but he wasn't bright enough to trick Julian or hand him in either. He would be some use as a getaway driver. Running out of options and always a man of resource, Julian had turned to the one person who, in some body or another, had always helped him: his woman. If things had cooled down and Electra had decided to leave Julian would have waited to build rapport with another girl and probably got bored of the idea before he had enough people to go through with the heist. The night she left he had reloaded his dating profile and called a couple of his other dealers. He usually just went out with his old dealer girls due to the rapport they had already built with him, but he was open to new possibilities. There was nothing some women wouldn't do for an intelligent bad boy, as Julian had found since middle school.

The heist was a perfect plan. Electra would distract the cashier during the quiet time of day, when everyone else was upstairs having lunch or outside smoking. Julian insisted she should go as far as she had to in order to keep him distracted. She was hesitant, but somehow he persuaded her. Then again, money was persuasive. She flirted with the cashier for an hour until everyone else had left and he was the only member of staff there. Meanwhile, Julian used the scaffolding to slip past the cameras. The vault was locked, but, as he suspected, the combination method hadn't changed. They just moved the digits around on a monthly basis. Julian went through his old notes and over a few drinks and joints he worked out what the current combination must be. And he was right. He filled two sports bags with as much money as they could hold. Feeling an impulse of greed he also filled his parka and tightened it around the neck and waist.

Somehow he managed to evade the cameras and the staff in his suspicious getup. He made his way to Rocky's car and unloaded the money into the boot as inconspicuously as he could manage. Then he waited in the passenger seat for Electra to appear. After waiting half an hour, she emerged with her hair in a mess and a suspicious smile on her face.

Julian was pretty sure he saw her at the cashier as he was leaving, so if she had stayed behind to do anything else, it was on her. He was expecting her to hop into the car as though nothing happened, but instead she just walked up to it.

"Look babe, I'm gonna go and see a movie, OK? I'll see you back at the house and we can discuss business later."

Julian rolled his eyes. "Sure babes. You could have told us."

Electra shrugged. "I just decided now. If it went well I'd go see a movie, if it didn't, well, I wouldn't, would I?"

"Fine, fine, but we already look suspicious as fuck. Go watch the movie. We'll count the... green and then you can get your cut when you're back."

Electra thought it over. She knew Julian would probably take an extra cut, but she really couldn't care less. As long as she had enough for a nice little house somewhere sunny, she was happy. She slung her bag higher up her shoulder, shrugged again as a sort of farewell and made her way to the cinema.

She didn't know she was being followed.

It hadn't been long before the workers had returned from their smoke and noticed the open vault. They called the police immediately. Paul Sanchez wasn't on duty, but as he parked his car he realized the last report to be radioed in was right opposite his house. But Paul had better things to do. He pretended not to notice and walked towards the door before remembering he had forgotten to get milk. As he turned sharply and walked down the street, a beautiful woman caught his eye. Electra wasn't exactly stunning or a great dresser, but she had that foxy redhead appeal that, when an expert eye landed on it, would turn heads. And Paul was an expert on redheads. He looked her up and down and saw her calmly walk towards the cinema. It couldn't hurt.

Feeling a little sheepish and ashamed of his actions, he quickly crossed the road and, after seeing what room Electra walked into, he bought a ticket. He always used to think of it as odd when young women watched action films but he was finding that, as of late, it was far more common. He sat one row behind her and stared at her hair through the commercials. A deeper investigation revealed it to be dyed, but that didn't matter any more. She was lovely and he spent the movie wondering how to approach her.

Fortunately for him, he didn't need to. With images of the money floating in her head, Electra could taste freedom already and was getting frisky for a fresh man. And with his dark Latin looks and stylish hair and shirt, Paul Sanchez fit the bill: he was her type. She spied him as she was packing her remaining snacks into her bag and impulsively left her number with him. Wordlessly, she left the cinema feeling warm and excited to the pit of her stomach.

Sanchez couldn't believe his luck. He was too nervous and confused to call her that night and decided to play it cool and put it off a few days. That was, until the next day he was assigned the case and discovered that one of the people they were trying to contact was his buxom redhead. She was suspected as an accomplice in bank robbery and either first or second degree murder of a cashier. He was in two minds as to whether to tell anyone, but he figured his job was more important than a possible fling with a potential criminal. He reported to Detective Carl Kenty with the fortunate information. Apparently she had been seen in the bank and outside the bank talking to their prime suspects: a man with dark hair and a pale complexion and a huge man with a farmer's tan and a tattoo on his left arm. Paul was hoping he'd be asked to contact her, but once all the details came out Kenty, destroyer of parties and champion of chastity, instead set Paul Sanchez, Rick McAllister and Paddy "Irish" Dola on watch at her house should the other two suspects appear. Paul would meet up with her at her home and the other two would watch. After all, they would likely bolt at any chance of police intervention and the woman, if she was an accomplice, would bolt just as much as the men. They needed to find her and watch her until she and her associates tried to do a runner. Then they would just have to follow them and catch the marked notes.

As planned, Paul called Electra's number and arranged a date. It was surprisingly easy, making him question whether it was a scam of another variety. Then again, as he was backed by Rick and Paddy, he felt fairly safe entering her home. All it would take was the press of a button and they'd receive an alert that he was in danger and be able to rush the house.

He needn't have worried. Electra invited him into the flat easily and with clear intentions. Not wanting to break his character, or at least that would be what Kenty heard, Paul followed her upstairs for the sort of lovemaking he had never imagined could exist in real life. He thought to himself what a pity it would be if this woman turned out to be an aggressive bank robber. What a pity if she were to go to prison for five, ten, twenty years. What a waste of natural charm and talent.

After he excused himself, he returned to where the others were and added himself to the night-watch rota. Paddy, ever paranoid, was certain something had to go wrong soon. It was all too smooth, too steady. It made no sense. They would hit a snag eventually and he would be there to tell everyone he told them so. Rick told Paddy to mind his work and leave everyone else alone, at which Paddy retreated to standard grumbling.

Later that evening, when Paul was on duty and feeling certain any woman would avoid the dark cover of the barely lit streets, Electra emerged from the flat. She had a note in one hand and her car keys in the other. Paul was confident that nobody else could be home, so wherever she was going, it was likely the other robbers were as well. If she was part of the robbery, that was. As she turned the corner, he ignited the engine and creeped the car behind hers, keeping close but leaving enough space for doubt. Not that there was much point. The streets were so bare that if she paid any attention to him she would notice he was following her. He just hoped she wouldn't, or she wouldn't think anything of it.

But those streets were pretty familiar to him. And the more she drove, the more familiar they became. She was driving towards the bank and back to the scene of the crime. In his head, Paul formulated all sorts of clever reasons why she would return. They left something? That was their meet up point? Maybe it was true that the criminal always returned.

But Electra was driving that way for an entirely different reason. Paul hadn't noticed it, but she had watched him from a café as he made his way home the other night. She had seen the house where he lived and she had seen the police vehicle outside the door. When after their passionate lovemaking she spied him sneaking into a pretty obvious surveillance vehicle opposite her, she had no doubts. Paul was a copper, a police officer, and on her tail in more ways than she was on his.

She had mulled it over. He may be a police officer, but he was very good looking and very charming. She liked their smalltalk and that they shared tastes in music and films. As an upstanding member of the community with a safe job, he was a promising prospect, unlike a certain person. She was determined to make this work somehow.

So she pulled up by his house, stepped outside the car and leaned against his house door. At that point Paul realized what she had been doing. She wasn't returning to the scene, she was returning to him. And branding him a policeman by doing so.

He wasn't sure whether to park and step out or to avoid her entirely, but as her carefully manicured fingernail beckoned him he knew he had no choice. He parked and made his way over to his own house and the dangerous redhead in front of it.

"I knew it, Paulie." She grinned, impressed with herself. "You're police, aren't ya?"

Paul nodded, wincing slightly at the newly-acquired nickname.

"I bet you're after Julian. I should have known he couldn't make good of something like this…" His raised eyebrow caught her eye before he could mask it. "You don't know?"

"Ma'am, cooperating with the police could save you a lot of jail time."

Electra laughed and nodded. "I know, I know. But if you know nothing, you prove nothing."

"Technically I am on duty, so I can use what you say. It would be my word against yours."

Electra smiled widely. "I guess so." She wasn't sure where to go from there. She desperately wanted to spill her guts to Paul and make passionate love to him in his own bed that very instant. He was the sort of man that inspired the deepest heat in her, like Julian had been until he proved his weak character and slovenly nature. But that heat rarely turned out well. If she walked away from the money now and walked into Paul's arms, he could turn out to be another Julian. Then what of her little house in the sun, of her early retirement surrounded by tan pool boys and elite women for continual intellectual and physical stimulation? She would get neither and wind up a spinster. It might be an old-fashioned concept, but the very thought of remaining poor and single into old age tightened her stomach. There was only one way.

"Say, Paulie." She cooed. "Do you find me attractive?"

"I am on duty." Paul reminded her, his eyes scanning her wildly curved figure. "I don't think I need to remind you."

"You were on duty last time you seduced me too." She smirked. "Why can't I seduce you while you're on duty?"

"I suppose I find you attractive." Paul confessed. "Extremely attractive, in fact."

"And do you find money attractive, Paulie?" She continued.

"Everyone finds money attractive, Electra." He smiled back at her. He knew she was going nowhere good, but he was happy to entertain her in case she made another slip like before. Though, in the rush, he had somehow forgotten the name. Willie? Jailer? Wally? He wasn't sure any more. Her curves were doing their magic on him. He forced his eyes to the wall just behind her.

"Then I have an idea." Electra grinned. "How about you help me get the money and I help you get me and the money?"

"And how would that work?" Paul forced the smile to stay put.

"The mastermind behind this whole operation was Julian. He is currently my partner, though Heaven knows I don't want him to be. The only reason I went along with this was because I figured I'd never get caught, but now I'm getting shit for it and he isn't, which is hardly fair. I propose this: you kill Julian. I can give you the address, make it look like it was in the line of duty of whatever you coppers call it. I collect the money. You claim it was already gone and I had nothing to do with it. We both disappear to Barbados and live out our lives under the sun, fucking like rabbits and drinking away our retirement."

Paul was disgusted. At every single aspect of the situation. He was disgusted that Electra already had a partner and was so readily spreading her legs for new men. He was disgusted that she was staying with Julian for the money. He was disgusted that she wanted to kill her partner. He was disgusted that she wanted him to kill for sex and money. He was disgusted at the whole proposition.

"No thank you." He couldn't even bring himself to pretend he would do it. He just wanted to get home and have a cold shower to wash every last trace of her from his body. He pushed past her and opened the door, making his way upstairs.

Electra had reached to grab his buttocks as he walked past but thought better of it. The man didn't want her. She had already said too much and she wasn't sure what would happen if she did anything else. She watched him longingly before bolting home like a deer startled by a car.

The next morning Rock and Julian were round to talk cash. Despite his greedy arms, Julian had only managed to grab one million and a bit. As Julian and Electra argued over the money and how they would split it, Rock assumed his normal position at Electra's window.

He knew Julian was holding out on Electra: they had broken two million. But he also felt Electra deserved it and besides, he had been paid extra to keep his mouth shout and he wasn't a fool. So he left them squabbling and watched Ann through the window, as he usually did. Ann was Electra's neighbor and a mighty attractive girl at that. Rock had spied her one afternoon as he dropped off a bag of weed for Electra to sell and he'd been fascinated ever since. She kept her windows open during the day and often spent whole afternoons in the garden. She was the girl next door type he'd always liked. He'd never really given himself a chance to dream about these things, but now he knew he would be getting eight hundred thousand he felt happier about these dreams. He would have a strawberry field of his own somewhere nice and isolated. And he'd pay his workers a fair wage and overcharge the hippies that wanted organic strawberries. And on his arm he'd have a nice girl like Ann. Maybe even Ann herself. She was a joy to watch. He couldn't get her off his mind.

Paul, on the other hand, couldn't get Electra off his mind for another reason. He wasn't sure what at all to say to Kenty, so he filled it in on his own. He explained he hadn't seen either of the suspects around her and that she had revealed nothing. He was hoping that she would just disappear from his life. Or at least he was on the surface. Internally, a passion he never recalled experiencing before was boiling over. Electra was his perfect woman, the ideal. She had the figure, the flaming red hair and the sexy, fiery temperament. They even shared taste in music and films. She was his dream girl and the longer he spent trying to forget her, the less he could.

Relationships had never went the way Paul Sanchez wanted them to. Ever since middle school, like Julian, Paul had enjoyed girls' attention for his good looks. But unlike Julian Paul had never had a relationship last. Girls and women were drawn in by his dark locks and smoldering gaze, but almost instantly drew away from him. It was as though there were some part of him, some invisible feature that girls discovered in his bare soul. He tried being standoffish. He tried being nice. He tried committing and cheating. And whatever he did, they just moved away. He had come to give up on a stable relationship at all, drifting from girl to girl, continually longing for one to stay, to validate his efforts, to make him feel loved. But none did. They wanted him, but they didn't love him. And he was starting to believe they couldn't.

At least until he met Electra. He saw how different she was. She desired him deeply. She shared enough with him. She was a voraciously sexual being as well as a fragile, emotional woman. She was everything he had been raised to believe a good partner should be. And maybe that was the missing component? Maybe she was just the right woman for him, the one he would have to be with?

He tried to shake the thought but the more he shook it the more it stuck. He became terrified of losing her. He found himself imagining her long legs around his waist, her hand on his thigh as they watched a film, her lips to his ear, whispering sweet nothings... And he was going to throw all this away because of a job? Because he wanted to be a good policeman? He'd tried being good. He'd tried being nice. And what had it got him? A standard salary, a small house and the single life. On the other hand, being bad, being criminal... that would get him his dream girl, his one and only, as well as more money than he was likely to make his entire life.

Paul had to do something. Or she might get away. Desperate, he took advantage of his day off and went to visit Electra. He was as secretive as he could be and he was glad about it too. Outside the house, still watching intently, was Rick in the police car. Clearly the front door wasn't an option, so, trying to stay hidden from the pretty girl in the garden opposite as well as from Rick's perfect vantage point, Paul slipped between the fences and down towards Electra's shared garden. Once there he tried looking for the red bohemian curtain he remembered from their lovemaking. The thoughts were still fresh in his mind and he quickly identified the window. He messaged her asking her to let him in. The window slid ajar and he clumsily made his way up the fire escape and slipped right in.

Electra was alone again. She wasn't about to tell Paul that Julian and Rock had just left the way he came or that she knew about the car still outside her house. She wasn't going to help him, however daringly romantic this gesture was.

Paul couldn't help himself and before he managed to utter even a whisper of the plan, he had her beneath him in the bed and he was breathing a sigh of relief into the kiss. She was a sweet aphrodisiac, a drug, an ambrosia. He needed her. Pulling his head back, he looked her straight in the eye. "I'll do it."

"Your mate outside isn't in on this, is he?" Electra was already suspicious.

Paul shook his head. "He doesn't even know I'm here. I've been doing some thinking and Barbados sounds sweet."

Electra smiled. "Good. You just missed Julian and the gang." For some reason, even though Rock was the only other one involved, she always thought of him as the gang.

"Will they be back?"

Electra nodded. "Yeah. Julian is dropping off my money around ten tonight. I think he's holding out on me. Probably on Rock too. That dim shit doesn't know left from right. You can stay here and follow him home. Then kill him at the door and call your cop buddies. Get the safe out the window, then say there was nothing."

"Are you sure this will work?"

Electra shrugged, not giving Paul much hope. "It'll work long enough to get us to Barbados, Paulie."

"What about Rick?"

She shrugged again. "I'll distract him. He's watching me after all. I can just walk off and he'll follow like a puppy. Then you can track Julian easily and nobody will notice either of you."

Paul nodded. "I sure as fuck hope this plays out as you think it will."

"It will, Paulie, it will."

They sat back and watched films and TV reruns as they waited for ten to arrive. This confirmed what Paul had been suspecting: that Electra was his dream girl, the ideal, who would be by his side forever. He was certain of it. It had to be fate. He held her close and counted his blessings. If there was justice in the world, he would pull off the killing and they would be able to live happily together somewhere where nobody would ever discover what they had done.

Soon Julian messaged Electra to say he was on his way. Electra kissed Paul and looked him in the eye as she promised him it would all work out. Paul was quickly bundled into the wardrobe as Electra questioned herself and her choice in men again. Was Paul really right for the job? Could she trust him? The idea was that she would get her money off Julian, see him off then rush out to distract Ricky as Paul followed Julian home. It seemed like a sensible plan to her, but she still had her questions. She hoped Paul could actually go through with it and finish Julian and hand the vault out the window. She hoped she could make it there after losing Ricky. She hoped Rock wouldn't still be there. She hoped nobody would suspect a thing. It was all very difficult. She calmed down by telling herself that, should it all go to waste, she could always just play the "vulnerable chick card" and try and get out of it by pushing the blame onto the men. A gang ringleader and a corrupt police officer fighting it out wouldn't exactly sound wrong to anyone. And she would be safe.

She greeted Julian and tried to keep her face looking as sour as possible as she accepted the money and shouted at him about the cut she'd got. She shouted at him about how she'd had to service and then kill the cashier to keep everything running smoothly. Julian slapped her, as she expected him to, and she went silent and said something about going out to buy cigarettes. She left and Julian slipped back out the window. There was nothing more she could do. She wandered towards the store, knowing Ricky was on her heel. There was no way he could suspect the people sneaking in and out the windows. There was no way he could guess that his coworker was in cahoots with her. The plan was flawless. All Paul had to do was fire a couple of shots and blame it on Julian, which would be easy as Julian was an armed bank robber with a house full of weed.

Paul saw it as less clear cut. This shooting would be a lot of paperwork in the very best case scenario. Electra was worth it for the trouble, but he was hoping for a very fast getaway. Especially after hearing that she was the killer. Of course, she could have been making noise, saying anything to get a rise out of Julian... but he suspected she wasn't. Electra was a killer. And he was about to become one as well.

He tracked the man all the way to a bungalow in a run-down neighborhood. The place was probably nice a while ago, but those days were long gone. Julian walked in and left the door ajar. Paul always understood that as a sign he had or was expecting company, but he couldn't be too sure. He crept up to the door and peered in. Coast clear.

But Julian was aware of the man on his trail. And he suspected that this man and Electra were working together. He had no idea of the rest of the plan, though. He did not know that Paul was a police officer. He did not know that Paul was armed. He did not know that Paul was not planning a robbery, but a killing. So Julian sat back and watched TV and waited for his would-be burglar to make an appearance. He knew he was there and he knew he could get him with a bat or a gun before he could try anything.

Paul wasn't sure what to make of it. He spied through the crack of the door and soon noticed something was amiss. Julian was too obvious. Too ready. He knew someone or something was coming and he was prepared. Paul wouldn't be able to dodge this one. Julian was ready for him. He just needed to ask himself exactly what Julian felt he was ready for. For a policeman? Possibly. For a murderer? Possibly. For a robber? Possibly. For all three? Almost certainly not.

Paul braced himself. This would be the only way to do it. He stood upright and pushed the door open, gun in hand, finger on the trigger.

As Julian leaped up and brandished his own weapon, Paul knew that was all it would take. He fired three shots into Julian's chest. And then the man was down in a pool of his own blood. He hadn't expected Paul to be armed or ready to kill. And it had cost him. Paul cautiously checked Julian's pulse. He was dead. Next, he investigated the room. At first he was hit by the worry that it wouldn't work out, that the money or the safe weren't there. But he found the safe eventually and pushed it out the back window, as Electra asked him to, before calling Ricky to ask for backup. He had found a suspect, been assaulted and had to fire shots. The man was dead and they would need to be there as soon as possible.

What Paul didn't know was that the plan hadn't gone as smoothly as he and Electra had planned. Ricky hadn't been the only person observing Electra's house. Paddy had been planted further down the street and, while he hadn't seen Julian's initial visit, he had definitely seen the second visit along with Paul's less than stealthy exit after Julian.

Paddy was a man to stick to his job above everything else. He may be a touch paranoid and the other officers mocked him mercilessly for it, but it was born of a strong survival instinct and almost pathological perfectionism. He always needed everything to go smoothly so he always expected the worst. Needless to say, he hadn't foreseen this at all. Not that Paul would betray them like that. Or run his own completely illicit investigation. Paul had always been as by the books as Paddy was. But this didn't disappoint Paddy. He couldn't be disappointed. He expected the worst of everyone. So he had calmly followed Paul to Julian's house and watched as Paul spied on Julian. He wanted to know what Paul would do next and he had little reason to call anyone yet. After all, if Paul could arrest Julian it would save everyone time and Paddy's faith in humanity would have been slightly restored.

But it wasn't to be. He heard Paul fire gunshots. Then silence. Concerned, Paddy sneaked up as close to the window as he could and tried to look in. Paul was moving something heavy right towards him, though fortunately not looking at the window at that particular moment. Paddy moved to the side just as a large safe landed by his feet. This was gold. Not literally, but it was gold. This was all he needed. Then, as he heard Paul leave the bungalow, Paddy got the radio message that Paul would need backup due to a surveillance plan gone wrong.

At first Paddy wasn't sure what to do. He was the closest officer. But would his closeness be suspect? What if Paul worked out what had happened? Then again, he had to know. Paddy couldn't be certain that Paul was acting selfishly. Maybe it was all with good reason.

Gathering his courage, Paddy reported to the front of the bungalow, where Paul waited. Paul didn't seem shocked at what was happening. Paddy radioed that everything was under control before turning to Paul.

"So... What exactly happened here?"

Paul was a little surprised that Paddy was there, but he wrote it off as that they were all hot on Julian's tail. "I was following this man, I thought he was Harry Julian, a suspect."

Paddy raised an eyebrow. "But you were off duty?"

Paul nodded. "A policeman is never off duty."

Paddy smiled. "And you managed to track him? How did you work out where he was?"

"I just figured it out."

"What if I were to tell you that I saw it all?" Paddy revealed. "Could you be more honest with me then?"

Paul had not anticipated this. Anything else he was prepared for, but not this. "You saw it all?"

Paddy nodded. "I'm sure your behavior can be explained. How you came to be in Electra's house, why you followed Harry Julian out the back."

But Paul couldn't explain it. He didn't think he would have to and he was at a loss. There would be no negotiating with Paddy, no making secret arrangements for a portion of the money. The best he could do

would be distract him until Electra had collected the money and then...
Then what? Paul knew what he had to do. He just didn't want to.
Killing a criminal in the line of work was one thing. But killing another
officer to cover up a crime? A crime he had committed for another
criminal, so they could both run away, nonetheless. He wasn't sure he
had it in him.

Paul wondered whether Electra could get away without him.
Probably not. She needed to be clear.

Electra was soon there and noticed the police officer in front of
Paul. She froze and watched them. Could Paul be trying to betray her?
But no, Paul was guiding the officer away. She wasn't sure she could
trust him any more. Why could she never trust the people she needed
to trust? But from the hill she could also see the safe that had been
pushed out the window. If there was any chance of getting it before
Rock got it, before the officers returned or before Ricky was back on
her tail, it was now.

Electra walked calmly down the street, keeping an eye on the car up
the road where Paul and the other, uniformed officer were talking. They
didn't look her way. She moved round the back of the building and
opened the safe. There was a lot more than the four hundred thousand
Julian had claimed he had. It was quite likely that was all there was,
that he'd made one and a half million like they had planned. It was also
possible that they'd made even more and Rock already had his share.
But Electra wasn't bothered. She moved the money into her shopping
bags and purse and calmly walked back the way she came. Nobody
would notice a thing.

Paddy hadn't noticed her. Paul had been watching the safe and was
very grateful when Electra appeared, emptied it, locked it again and
disappeared. There was one fear that remained in her mind: would she
do a runner with the money? Or did she love him, would she wait?

Someone else who had witnessed the incident was Rock. He had
been staying at a friend's flat across the road, looking down on the

whole row of bungalows. He had seen Julian being stalked, he had heard the shooting and he had seen Electra collect the money. But he wasn't too bothered. It served Julian right, for messing with a woman like that. He wanted out of it now. He'd spent too much time out in the open, committing crimes and staying away from honest work. He would use his money to buy himself a flat and learn a trade, take on an apprenticeship in IT or something equally promising. Then he could sell the flat and move somewhere in the country, work from home and own his strawberry field. It would all come together. He wasn't ready to get caught yet. He just had to lay low until it all blew over.

So he just leaned on the window sill, knowing the light reflecting off the glass was hiding him, sipping his beer and chatting to his friend about something and nothing, watching Electra walk away with the money as the cops bickered. Rock didn't get how both those cops had missed Electra. Surely one of them had seen her sneak round the back and empty the safe? But they were too busy arguing.

Then, through the glass, Rock faintly heard another shot fired. The uniformed officer fell to the ground. Rock raised an eyebrow but sighed. There was no point calling anyone or getting involved. It was too dangerous. He walked towards the kitchen and got himself another beer.

Paul didn't know how he had managed it. One moment he and Paddy were arguing about the situation and Paul's apparent over involvement. The next, Paul had shot Paddy in the gut and the head. It wasn't instinct. But he didn't even remember pulling out the gun, removing the safety and pulling the trigger. Paddy hadn't expected it at all. He hadn't even taken out his own gun. He just lay there, a crumpled form, like he had fallen asleep in an awkward position.

Paul didn't know what to do. He had killed a policeman and backup would soon follow. The only thing he could think of was to move the body. It would be discovered, but it could buy them some time to escape. This was a pretty bad area. Shootings were common, killings were common. Nobody would question another police officer's body, some extra shots or a car.

Clumsily, Paul heaved Paddy's body into the car. There was little blood underneath him, so it probably wouldn't be noticed. The best way of getting rid of it would be to drive him somewhere else. But that would be too suspicious. Instead, Paul looked down the hill. It was still quite steep. The car should roll back fast. Leaning in, he pulled the hand break and watched the car roll off before he made his way back to Electra's flat.

Electra was there, counting her money. Ricky's car had been nowhere to be seen, although after the incident with Paddy, Paul couldn't be too sure any more. Electra, despite the fact she had just had her ex boyfriend killed and probably knew about Paddy, was bubbly and happy. She didn't care about these deaths, about these crimes. Three people's blood was on her hands, but it didn't particularly bother her. She was just happy it was going so smoothly, that she was getting the money.

"We did it, Paul. We have a cool million and a half now. All ours. We can go to Barbados and buy a nice house on the beach."

Paul nodded.

Electra sensed he wasn't all that happy with the arrangement any more, but that didn't matter. He wasn't going to betray her. Worst case scenario, she could leave him here to get caught. "Did you get rid of the other officer?"

Paul nodded again. "Yes. Paddy's gone, but we're going to have to get moving soon."

Electra raised an eyebrow. She wasn't quite sure what Paul meant.

"You can't kill a policeman at a crime scene when people know where you are. It means they will find you. They know your flat and they know me. We need to go."

Electra sighed and stood up, stretching so her back cracked. "I guess so. You go get your shit and find us a motel. Here's some cash.

When you have it, come and collect me in the morning. Then we can book our flight and fuck off to Barbados."

"Do you even have a passport?"

Electra nodded. "I've been planning on getting away from Julian for a while now. Anyhow, you need to get home, get your shit together and get to a motel. They know you were there, but nobody knows I was involved here and I want it to stay that way."

Paul nodded back. "I get you. See you tomorrow."

"See you tomorrow." Electra kissed him deeply, a hint of what was to come for the rest of his life. Almost all his worries, concerns and anger faded away. He would do anything for Electra. He would kill, rob and skip the country to Barbados. She was worth it all.

As Paul left her flat, he made sure nobody was watching it. Rick still wasn't back and there was no sign of anyone else. They were probably busy at the crime scene. He needed to get his things before anyone suspected him or went to his house. Which would be soon. He waved at Electra's neighbor as he walked past and she smiled and waved back before going inside.

As he suspected, his flat was not under surveillance, but he had a few missed calls on both his mobile and his landline. Then he worked out what was happening. He had been there and killed Julian in the line of duty. Paddy had joined him. Paddy's body was down the road, bleeding out into his crashed car. And there was blood all over the bungalow and the street. They suspected Paul had been killed or kidnapped. Thinking fast, Paul tried to not make his flat look much different. He grabbed some money but left his wallet. He grabbed a couple of forms of ID but left his birth certificate. He took some very old clothes and some food and threw it all into an old bag before escaping.

He locked the door and put on a hooded coat. Then, he took a taxi to the highway and stopped at the first motel. Everything was perfect. His car wouldn't move. His body wouldn't be found. He could leave a note on Electra's door saying she had ran away and that she and some thugs had kidnapped him to make themselves safe. It would buy them even more time. He texted her the details and she agreed it sounded good.

If he was a hostage then nobody would suspect anything. They could get away safely and nothing would interfere. Paul went to sleep feeling comfortable in the knowledge that they were getting away to Barbados in a matter of days.

Ricky arrived at Paul Sanchez's door and found it locked, just as Paul would have left it. They had already worked out someone had used Paul's gun to kill Paddy and were fearful for Paul's life and safety. But the girl, Electra, had simply returned home from shopping and there was no sign she had been anywhere near there. Besides that, no woman her size would have so easily lifted the safe and hauled it out the window. Perhaps the thugs that followed Harry Julian and his gang had finally come back for what they wanted, what they felt they deserved. They money had been gone. Whoever came for it either knew the combination to the safe or was sorely disappointed.

Ricky had managed to get permission to investigate Paul's flat. He broke down the door and found it empty. Everything was as Paul would have left it: a complete mess. Food in the fridge, his wallet on the side. That should have calmed any suspicions Ricky had. But it didn't. Because Paul's car keys were on the side, his driver's license was missing and his voice mail had been accessed. Of course, it could all be innocent. But Ricky suspected that someone had been there. Someone who shouldn't have been. Maybe a criminal, maybe Paul himself. And they didn't want anyone to understand what was happening. They knew how to hide such matters from the police. But they didn't know how to hide Paul's nature from his long-time coworker.

When Ricky got back to headquarters he found Kenty was a little behind on the news. Kenty was still following an old lead that Julian had been sighted near the flat. Paddy's old lead. Of course, the information was useful: Julian had visited Electra. But it wasn't grounds for anything yet. They needed a search warrant to get into her house and they were pretty sure they wouldn't get one.

Ricky updated Kenty on the deaths: Julian, Paddy and possibly Paul. Kenty shook his head. "Two fine young officers." Ricky hadn't the heart to suggest what he suspected. After all, chances were he was over analyzing anyway. How likely was it that Paul had anything to do with it? More likely was that they dragged him home and took his passport so they could hop the border with him. Maybe he left his keys as a sort of sign that Ricky would be able to follow. All that was more likely than Paul being somehow involved.

That night, Kenty released a press bulletin explaining that a few people had died and a valuable officer was still missing. He urged anyone with any information whatsoever to come forward as soon as possible.

Paul was asleep in his motel room bed already. Dreaming about waking up in silk sheets with Electra wrapped around his body and the sea lapping the wall around their house during high tide.

Electra was sat up, smoking and drinking and packing her bags, trying to keep it to two cases although one was full of money, hidden by clothes and cookware. She didn't watch the news and wasn't in the mood for TV anyway, as her paranoia was setting in.

Rock didn't own a television and was sat up drinking beer on his own at his own place, having just returned from his friend's house. He was pondering how to stay out of the police's way until it all blew over.

But Ann saw the bulletin. She wasn't a dedicated watcher of the news, but she enjoyed having some sound in the background as she went about her chores. She had been an earnest worker since early childhood, when her mother had died and her father took over caring for the six children. He would bring home the money and she would clean and cook and make sure everyone was ready for school every day. Despite the odds they had done very well and Ann worked only mornings at a local office, leaving her plenty of time to garden, cook and socialize. But she would still stay up late to finish her chores, do the laundry and maybe read a book. And as she was ironing her shirts for the next day she had the news on in the background.

The bulletin didn't mean much to her. She knew there had been a robbery a while back and that earlier in the afternoon they had found the ringleader's body. And good riddance too. She wasn't glad of his death, but she was glad he had been found. The news that there were more gang members, some armed thugs that had rebelled against their leader and kidnapped a policeman, made her shake her head. She was an old soul and couldn't help but feel that in times gone by these things just didn't happen.

But she did remember seeing the police officer somewhere before, the missing man. Of course, he had been wandering the street a few days ago, possibly on the hunt for any criminal activity going on in the flats opposite. She knew the woman who lived there in the second floor was a drug dealer and that the ground floor was home to some prostitutes. So she wasn't surprised that a police officer would be round there. But no, that wasn't quite it. She couldn't remember, but she had seen him somewhere and she seriously couldn't remember where.

As she lay in bed, thoughts danced in front of her eyes. But she didn't put them together until the next morning.

Paul made his way to Electra's house under the cover of dawn. The taxi pulled up outside, but even though she had replied to his text by saying she was getting up, she was nowhere to be seen. He texted her again and she still didn't reply. He asked the cabbie to wait for them and went upstairs to hammer her door down. He had heard on the radio on the drive down that the police were asking people to come forward and seeking warrants for various houses, which probably included Electra's. They needed to get her out of there and leave the note on the door.

Paul had scribbled a ransom note on the motel paper and was planning on sticking it to the door to be found by Ricky. Electra had not, as she had told him, been getting up and was still nude. However much he wanted to ravish her then and there, he explained the situation and Electra got dressed quickly. But not quickly enough. As they taped the note to the door and darted downstairs, Paul realized the cab had driven away, probably not desiring to stay in a slightly bad area more than a few minutes. He knew he shouldn't have paid the man in advance. Paul's belongings were still at the motel, so that much was safe, but they had to call another taxi and wait on the curb.

As Ann walked around the house opening the upstairs windows before she went to work, she spied Paul and Electra out of the corner of her eye.

The night before she had vaguely remembered his face, but now there was no mistaking it. Electra's handsome visitor was the missing policeman. Ann didn't know the ins and outs of the situation. And she didn't want to meddle with another person's private matters. But she also didn't want to not report Paul to the police. Stood by her window, she called them and explained what she saw.

Ricky, on the other end of the line, put two and two together. Even though he and Kenty had been up all night seeking a warrant, they raced to their car and asked Ann to wait inside until they arrived. The situation might be about to become dangerous.

Ann was happy to oblige, but after ten minutes Paul and Electra were still there. The police and the taxi were both stuck in the awful morning traffic and Ann was starting to worry about getting to work late. She grabbed her bag, put on her shoes and headed out the door. She smiled and waved at Paul and Electra as she got into her car and checked her bag to make sure she had everything.

It all happened at once. The police arrived before the taxi did. Paul spied them and grabbed Electra, who grabbed her bag of money. They darted towards Ann's car. Ann couldn't bring herself to start it or run into them. In a matter of seconds, Paul, Electra and the bag were in the back behind her and Paul was pressing a gun to the back of her head.

"Drive. Highway. Now."

Ann nodded. She felt frozen, but she knew what she had to do. Somehow keeping her cool, she started the car and made her way towards the motorway.

Paul didn't know what he was doing any more. Someone had got a search warrant for the house or someone had tipped off the police and now they were after him. They had seen him and Electra patiently waiting for their taxi on the curbside. They had seen him take a hostage. It was too late. They were in too deep. He needed to evade the police, get the bag from the motel and make his way to to the airport where he and Electra could slip away. It would be fast and then it would be over.

When they got to the motel, Paul grabbed Ann by the neck as he exited the vehicle, then pointing the gun through the window and asking her to get out. "I'm sorry." He apologized. "I don't want to hurt you. I just need to use you as... well, as a shield, so we can get away."

Ann shook her head, holding back tears. "Please don't do this. I have an elderly father to care for. I'm still young."

"I won't hurt you." Paul was getting more and more nervous. This had escalated far beyond what he was happy to work with. This was far too dangerous, far too much. He guided Ann into the motel, with Electra staying behind, a gun in her own hands, guarding her money with her life. Paul was in too deep now. He had killed a criminal and a police officer. He had betrayed the force and kidnapped an innocent woman. And he was on his way to Barbados with his dream girl.

His life couldn't be fixed here any more. He could only try and get away as fast as possible. He locked the door and made Ann sit on the bed as he checked he had everything. She was still almost crying. But he didn't know what else to do.

Everything was in the bag. Now all he had to do was... Ann's eyes were locked on the motel room window. Paul looked up. Ricky stood there, gun in hand. Without thinking, Paul took aim at Ricky. Ricky braced himself and fired two shots.

Paul felt a burning pain spread down his arm and through his chest. He had been hit through the lung and in the shoulder. He dropped the gun and collapsed. He wanted to be afraid of dying. He wanted to avoid it. But the fear was gone. He had thrown everything away. He pulled himself to his feet. Ann ran to the window, but he made no move to stop her. She was blocking Ricky's gun from delivering a fatal bullet.

Maybe there was still time? Maybe there was still a chance?

He staggered outside. Kenty stood outside, several officers around the car. Electra was standing beside it, gun in hand, scowling. She still wanted to get away. She knew she couldn't, but she was furious at how she had been set up, how she had been caught. She couldn't pretend it was all the guys now. It had gone too far. They knew.

She spied Paul staggering out of the main entrance and ran over to him, dropping her gun. It was all over. They weren't going to Barbados. They weren't keeping the money. No little house in the sun or handsome pool boys or busy shopping sprees in richly scented markets.

Paul collapsed over her shoulder as the policemen drew closer. His arm wrapped around her shoulder as he kissed her, his wounds pressing blood into her arm, shoulder and breast.

"Tell me..." He sighed. "Tell me, baby. Could we have had a chance without the money?"

He collapsed before she could answer. He was dead.

***

Rock walked around his new flat and looked out the window onto the garden. It was a nice place. He was glad it had come up for sale after Electra had gone to prison and her rent had expired. He wouldn't have wanted to rent it, after all. But owning it wasn't bad and with how inexpensive it was he could always rent it out once he moved and make a small income that way.

He, like everyone else, had heard about the case from the news in bars and the odd newspaper or magazine he'd read. He was surprised, but not shocked at how it had all come together. He had done well to lay low. Over the course of the few months in hiding he had carefully paid his money into his account, claiming to be a male escort. Nobody would try and trace a John for proof that he, or in his case she, had hired a prostitute. The plan had worked flawlessly and Rock was pretty impressed with himself. By eight months he had enough money to finish paying for the flat and move in. He would continue claiming he was a male escort until he had no more money to deposit.

The next move was less calculated. He couldn't force her, after all. But they had something in common and he hoped to bond over that. Despite everything she had been through, Ann was staying in her ground-floor flat opposite, still going upstairs to care for her elderly father in his flat, still working hard. Rock was impressed at her toughness and had used his old connection with Julian to flirt with her. She hadn't been shocked or scared and agreed to go on a few dates with him. They had already been to the cinema and he was planning on taking her to a fancy Greek restaurant the next evening. She "knew" he was an escort and didn't mind.

She was lovely. Pretty, non judgmental, hard working, a loving daughter and tough as nails. She was the sort of woman he wanted on his strawberry farm.

Rock waved at her out the window as she worked on her flower beds. He smiled lightly, a rare smile, as she blew him a kiss.

END

THE DARK SHIFT

SARAH LOWEY

It was innocent enough, to begin with when Bridie, Maddy, and Camila posted an ad on Craigslist for a new roommate. It was a simple act, as easy as the click of the mouse; yet, that simple act set in motion a dark string of events that would not only become a battle for survival but would test the mettle of their characters to the extreme. It didn't take long to get a response for the ad, albeit just one response. Camila took the call.

"She sounds great," Camila had gushed afterward. "She seems like a no-fuss kind of person; she should fit in really well."

And when she'd turned up for the interview, Bridie and Maddy couldn't help but agree. Their first impression of the girl could be summed up in one word – wholesome. Ever heard the phrase 'wholesome as apple pie?' Well, that was Faith. She was petite with soft, dark blonde hair and large, gray eyes in a heart-shaped face of peaches and cream. The only thing that marred the purity of her face was a faded bruise on her left cheek. Apart from that, she was perfect. She seemed cheerful and relaxed, just the right combination of friendliness and restraint. This girl, they thought, would be fun while still respecting boundaries. She also, had a month's rent to pay upfront which pretty much clinched the deal.

"How soon can you move in?" Bridie had asked.

"Today, if you'll have me?"

It didn't take her long to move in. In fact, everything she owned was in one black duffle bag, which seemed a little odd to the girls but they didn't like to pry. In a couple of hours, she was set up in the back room with the view onto the park that adjoined the rear of the apartment block. She was standing at the window a couple of hours later, gazing at that view with a faraway expression when Bridie knocked on her door holding a glass of Coke and a sandwich.

"I bet you could use something to eat," said Bridie. Faith started in surprise. "Oh, sorry, I was daydreaming." She took the sandwich gratefully. "Thanks for this. I could eat a horse."

Bridie sat down on the end of the bed and watched Faith who was trying not to wolf the food down too fast. How long had it been since her last meal? She shifted on the bed making herself comfortable.

"So, where do you come from?"

"Iowa," Faith answered between bites. "I'm from a small town called Barnaby's Creek which you've probably never heard of. My parents run an old-fashioned General Mercantile there," she paused and turned her face to the window, "I really miss them... I miss home." Her face took on the faraway look again and her voice cracked with emotion. Bridie's heart went out to her.

"I miss my family too," she confided, thinking of her own tousle-haired twin brothers, her burly big-hearted father, and her funny, strong minded mother. "You don't really understand what your family means to you until they aren't around anymore – but it does get easier, it really does."

Faith shook her head. "That's what I used to think. But I don't anymore. You never get over being away from the people you love."

Her words seemed loaded with meaning and Bridie wondered if there was more to Faith than her simple country-girl exterior suggested. Had she dealt with the death of a loved one? Was she a survivor of divorce? But before Bridie could ask her, they were interrupted by Maddy who exploded through the bedroom door with excitement.

"Party at Brad and Josh's tonight - 8 o'clock – everyone's going to be there!"

Camila poked her head over Maddy's shoulder. "What she means is that the cute redhead from French Lit class is going to be there."

Maddy grinned, nodding. "Hey, are you going to come too, Faith? It will give you a chance to get to know people and there will be plenty of cute guys to go around."

"No!"

Maddy, Camila, and Bridie stopped in surprise at Faith's outburst, sharing surreptitious glances with each other.

Faith seemed to gather herself and mumbled apologetically. "I'm sorry, I didn't mean to shout. It's just that I have panic attacks in new situations like that. If you don't mind, I'll take my time to get to know everyone. Besides, I'm tired and really need an early night..."

The girls rushed to console her. It was fine; there was no rush. There were parties every other week to attend. They left Faith to herself and got ready for the party which turned out to be particularly fun. In fact, they were having so much fun that Bridie didn't even think about Faith again until they pulled up around 2: a.m. at the front of their apartment block in Camila's beat up old 95 Honda Civic. Bridie and Camila were cackling with laughter at something stupid Maddy had said as they spilled out of the car. On the way down the garden path, Bridie slipped on something, falling flat on her behind with her legs flying up in the air. She lay on her back laughing helplessly while Camila and Maddy leaned on each other, laughing noiselessly at her misfortune.

"What the hell did I trip over?" hissed Bridie from the ground. "Quit laughing you guys!" Bridie, rolled clumsily onto her stomach taking the opportunity while she was still on the ground to flick on her phone light and scan the pathway. Something glinted in the grass.

"What's this?" she murmured, reaching over to pick it up. "Shhh! Will you guys be quiet?"

Maddy and Camila were still giggling as Bridie picked up the object and examined it. It was a pearl stud earring. There was something familiar about the earring which she kept it clutched in her hand as she scrambled to her feet. "Shhh," Bridie repeated, as she pushed Camila and Maddy towards the front door.

The stairwell was dark as a tomb making Bridie curse the Building superintendent for not fixing the broken light which had been broken for nearly a month. She stood huddled with Maddy and Camila at the bottom of the stairs. Their laughter had died out as soon as the front door had shut heavily behind them with an echoing blam, blanketing them in darkness.

Bridie found herself clutching the back of Camila's dress. It was so deadly quiet. Most of the other tenants in the apartment block were elderly and would almost certainly be asleep at this hour which normally, wouldn't have bothered her. It was nice to live near people who didn't get drunk and pee in the stairwell; nevertheless, right now it would've been nice to hear someone's television blaring or to be able to make out the glow of friendly light under someone's door.

Maddy, the least skittish of the three, began to climb the stairs ahead of Bridie and Camila but came to an abrupt stop at the top. She seemed frozen, statue-like on the landing.

"What is it?" Camila had slowed down, hesitant to take another step.

Maddy looked down at them with wide eyes. "Our front door is open."

Bridie froze in suspended animation, but Camila was already backing down the staircase towards her. "I'm not going in there," she stammered. "We should call the police."

Bridie stopped her in her tracks. "Wait, it should be okay. Faith is in there, remember? She probably just went out and was careless."

Camila's expression cleared. "Oh, that's right. I forgot about Faith." Immediately, her face darkened again. "But that's irresponsible of her," she said turning and heading back up the stairs.

At the top, Maddy waited for them before stepping cautiously towards their apartment door. It was wide open and the living room was in darkness. A dim light coming from the back of the apartment spilled into the hallway. Bridie moved to enter the apartment.

"Wait!" hissed Maddy, pulling her back. "I have a can of mace." She rummaged in her bag and produced a small black canister. "I've never had to use this thing before," she whispered, holding it out in front of her.

Together, as a group, they took one step through the doorway. Bridie reached out her hand in the darkness, sliding it up and down the wall until her palm ran over the switch. Light flooded the living room. Every cushion had been pulled off the sofa and ripped up; stuffing was lying all over the floor; the lampstand lay on its side, and magazines had been shredded and flung all over the room. Bridie staggered back, clutching the wall for support, Maddy swore under her breath and Camila crossed herself. "The little thief," she spat. "She burgled us!"

"We don't know that for sure, Camila," said Bridie, ignoring her friend's accusation. She took a step toward the hallway. "Faith, are you here?"

There was silence except for the second hand on the clock slotting into place, tick – tick – tick. Camila sidled back toward the open door. "There is no way I'm going any further. I'm calling the police." She fumbled with her phone and began dialing.

Maddy and Bridie took each other by the arm and started to take tentative steps down the hall towards Faith's room. Switching on the lights as they went, they could see that whoever had been there had ransacked their rooms as well. At the end of the hall, Faith's bedroom door was ajar a couple of inches. Dim lamplight glowed from within.

"Bridie, maybe we should wait for the police to get here before we look in Faith's room?"

Bridie, swallowed, she was scared too, but something compelled her to keep going. She didn't answer, Maddy, but allowed her feet to propel her forward. Maddy's breath was hot on her neck as Bridie reached out her hand and tapped the door with her fingers. Silently, the door swung open, revealing the bedroom turned upside down and inside out. Maddy and Bridie let out involuntary cries of anticipation. But their cries turned to gasps as they realized that the room was empty. No Faith. No serial killer lurking in the corner.

Bridie and Maddy fell into each other's arms with relief which was short-lived. If Faith wasn't here, where was she? What had she taken? Why did she ransack her own room? Was she the culprit or was there something more sinister going on? Out of the corner of her eye, Bridie saw something glinting on the floor near the curtain. It looked like an earring. She recognized it immediately because its twin was still clutched tightly in her hand. A pearl stud earring. Faith's earring. She showed Maddy.

"Looks like someone was in a hurry to get out of here," she muttered.

They made their way back to the living room waiting for the arrival of the police. Within ten minutes a pair of officers arrived. The ruckus had finally roused some of their elderly neighbors and a few sleepy, silver-haired heads peered between cracks in curtains and narrowly opened doors. After a quick search, it was established, oddly enough, that despite the effort taken to ransack the place, nothing had been taken.

The girls sat in a tight huddle on the sofa. While one police officer continued to collect evidence the other sat opposite the girls taking their statement. Her sharp black eyes taking everything in at once, her voice business-like and efficient. Officer Carol Blackthorne had twenty years' experience in the force under her belt.

"So, you say that before today you never met this girl?"

"Well, I spoke to her on the phone yesterday," answered, Camila. "But we met her in person for the first time today."

"Was there anything unusual about her behavior or appearance?"

"She's a really good actor," stated Maddy contemptuously. "She acted really nice and we got sucked in hook, line, and sinker."

"I noticed something." It was Bridie.

"Yes?" Officer Blackthorne's attention shifted to Bridie, pen poised in her hand. Bridie shifted in her seat.

"She had a faded bruise on her left cheek under her eye. As though she had been punched a while back. But she just didn't seem the type to get herself in trouble, you know? I just pushed the thought out of my mind."

Officer Blackthorne's stare was unwavering. "That's interesting you should say that. We put her name through a check and Faith Bellamy has come back as a missing person. She was reported missing by her family six months ago; did she say anything to indicate to you that might be the case?"

Bridie shrugged. "She told me she was from Iowa and she missed her family."

At that information, Officer Blackthorne's expression shifted almost imperceptibly. "Thank you, that will be all for now. We'll let you know if we find anything out. In the meantime, I'd suggest you get new locks for your door. Although I don't think this girl will be coming back, it's always better to be safe than sorry."

When the officers left half an hour later, the girls sat drinking hot chocolate on the sofa. Everyone was too shocked to sleep, nor did anyone feel like going to sleep in their messed-up rooms. The thought of a stranger touching their things was too unnerving to be conducive to peaceful dreaming. Eventually, blankets and pillows were pulled out to make simple beds in the living room where they talked in quiet tones before slipping into exhausted oblivion.

Bridie was woken by the sound of the McPherson's radio blaring. They were both deaf so they always turned the volume to max. It was so loud she could hear the talkback show they were listening to. Someone was calling up for advice on how to get rid of Aphids from their rose bushes.

"Shut up, nobody cares about your stupid roses," she mumbled grumpily into her pillow. It was a few seconds before the events of the previous night came flooding back and she sat up abruptly, blinking and yawning. Maddy was snoring like a lawn mower and Camila was invisible except for a tuft of black hair just visible under her blankets. Bridie allowed herself to slump back on her pillow, shutting her eyes against the light streaming through the curtains. With her eyes still closed, she felt for her phone and flicked it on.

Flashing on her screen was an unread text. Realizing she must have had her volume switched off, she quickly adjusted her settings and checked the text. It was from Faith. Curious, she rubbed her still gluggy eyes so she could see it better. The text was time coded at 11:18 p.m. the night before. Bridie's blood ran cold as the words, typed in hurried desperation, materialized before her eyes.

Shes comng for me Akuma

Im dead. Tell my mom and d

The text ended abruptly. Bridie felt the blood drain from her face as she imagined Faith lying dead somewhere or on the run from something or someone evil. Akuma? Who or what was that? Sleep suddenly the farthest thing from her mind. Bridie scrambled over the floor to wake Maddy. She showed her the text. Maddy snatched the phone from her, understanding dawning instantly on her face.

"Oh no, that poor girl!"

"We've got to let the police know. Maybe we're not too late."

"Let the police know what?" It was Camila, stirring from her bed.

Maddy showed her the text. "Bridie found this on her phone this morning. While we were at the party, poor Faith was running for her life from this... Akuma person."

Camila's eyes were as big as saucers. "You know what this means don't you? It means that some freaky dangerous person or people were in our house last night! We could be next! I wish we'd never laid eyes on that girl." She threw the phone into Bridie's lap in disgust.

"No, we'll tell the cops. They'll know what to do." Maddy stood up and was feverishly pacing the room, every now and then, checking out of the window as if she expected to see someone pulling up to the curb. "If we're in any danger they'll let us know."

Bridie's eyes went from Maddy's to Camila's. "Do you think we should try to call her?"

Maddy flopped down beside Bridie on the floor. "Are you crazy? If she's captured or dead, her killer might have her phone. Do you want her killer to know that we know something?"

Camila shuffled up closer to them so that they were sitting in a tight triangle on the floor. "They may have already seen Faith's text to you. They might already know that we know."

As the girls sat contemplating this unpleasant thought, there was a knock on the door. Nobody dared move. The door lock was still intact but the safety latch had been torn off its hinges the night before. Nobody was willing to pull the door open to see who was on the other side of the door.

Bridie gestured with her hands, indicating that she was going to look through the spy hole in the door. As she crept towards the door, the knock came again, this time more urgently. A quavering voice broke the silence from the other side.

"Yoohoo! Hello, anybody home?" Another knock. "Hello, girls. It's Edna from next door."

Bridie, Maddy, and Camila almost burst into tears with relief and Bridie quickly opened the door to reveal their 86-year-old, 4 foot nothing, neighbor.

"Hi honey," she beamed, craning her neck over Bridie's shoulder to try to get a look inside. "I sure hope everyone's o.k. I couldn't help but notice those nice police officers in your apartment last night." Her scant eyebrows were raised in question at Bridie.

"Thank you, Edna. We are all fine." Bridie didn't know how much or what to say. She certainly didn't want Edna to see the disarray behind her so she stepped forward half closing the door behind her. Edna looked up at her waiting hopefully for a titbit of gossip. Sighing, Bridie decided to go with a version of the truth. "Actually, the police were here to help us find a friend that seems to have gone missing."

Edna's bright button eyes perked up. "Oh, you must mean that dear little thing that came by my place about eleven o'clock last night. She was just darling and in such a rush! She gave me something to keep for you; said I was to give it to you first thing in the morning." At that, Edna stepped aside, pointing at something on the ground. Bridie's breath caught in her throat. There, lying on the ground at Edna's feet, was Faith's black duffle bag. She picked it up. There was something substantial inside by its weight.

"Thank you, so much, Edna," she said as she moved to go inside.

"It was my pleasure, honey," Edna smiled, hovering by the door, obviously in hope of being invited in. "If there's anything else I can help you with, you just let me know."

"I will." There was a brief, awkward silence at the end of which, Edna dolefully turned in the direction of her apartment. Bridie watched for a respectable amount of time as Edna moved off slowly down the hall before closing the door behind her. With the duffle bag, still, in her grasp, she turned to see Maddy's and Camila's wide-eyed faces staring at the bag in a mixture of fear and curiosity. They'd obviously heard everything. Without speaking, Bridie set the bag down on the floor between them.

"I'm too scared to open it." She whispered.

"I'm not." Maddy pulled the bag towards her and examined the bag. It had a zip with two heavy buckles. Each buckle was locked with a padlock. Undeterred, Maddy padded quickly to her bedroom. "I've got just the thing we need," she said over her shoulder. In a few minutes, she returned with a small black triangular object. "It's a padlock shim," she announced. "Nobody should be without one."

Bridie and Camila stared at Maddy in wonderment. They weren't about to question her on why she kept an implement for picking padlocks. Maddy's fingers trembled as she fitted the thin wedge around the shank of the first padlock and twisted. The shank popped open effortlessly. She moved to the second lock and did the same. Now all that was left between the girls and the contents of the bag was a zipper which was secured with a plastic zip-tie. Maddy used the shim to cut the tie.

"There," said Maddy with a tremor in her voice. "Who's going to open it?"

"You." Bridie and Camila said at once.

"Right then." Maddy took the zipper and dragged it open in one swift movement. The three girls let out a collective "Ohh," as the contents, bundles, and bundles of hundred dollar bills, spilled out of the bag.

"Money!"

"There must be at least a hundred grand here!"

"But why would she leave this with us?"

"This is what they must have been looking for last night."

They sat looking at one another, a hundred thoughts going through their heads. Maddy pulled the bundles of money off the top of the pile. Underneath, there was clothing and a notepad.

"Look, there's some of Faith's personal stuff here and a note."

Bridie opened the note scrawled in hurried writing.

Dear friends,

This money was made through evil means for an evil purpose. It was my intention to try to reverse the evil by using it for good. But I'm too late. Akuma has found me.

Please find my parents and tell them I love them and I did everything I could to find my way home. Perhaps it's better I didn't. At least if I'm dead she won't be able to trace me back to the people I love.

This money is in your care now. Do what you want with it.

Faith

Camila began to cry softly. "This is tragic. I can't bear it. What did this poor girl go through?"

Bridie's eyes roamed over the note. Although it was obviously written in a hurry, it was still measured in its message. "She must have written this before she sent the text. The text is much more desperate than this note."

"She wrote it while she was still here, obviously," continued Maddy. "Does it give any clue to where she would have been going?"

Bridie shook her head. A single tear slid down her cheek. All she could think of was Faith, terrified, frantic and alone against an enemy that she clearly believed she wouldn't be able to outrun. Akuma, whatever that was.

"Who or what the hell is Akuma?" Bridie asked the room at large. "Maybe it's some kind of gang or crime organization?"

"It sounds Japanese to me," said Maddy, typing the word in on a search engine on her phone. "Let's see if it means anything."

"You don't have to," interrupted Camila. "I've already found it." She turned the screen of her phone to face Maddy and Bridie. "This is what it means." Her face was pale and she looked ill.

Maddy and Bridie leaned forward to read the tiny writing on the English to Japanese translator. Japanese AKUMA = English DEMON.

"That's it!" Camila raised her palms in one emphatic movement. "I am not hanging around to find out what comes next in this saga. I don't want any of this dirty money and I don't want some psycho murderer to come chasing after me for it either!" She was starting to break down in tears again. Maddy moved close and tried to calm her, wrapping her arms around her soothingly.

"But that's just it, don't you see? Whoever Akuma is, they have already been here. They've already checked and found nothing. We aren't important enough to bother with and anyway, why would they come back here when, as far as they know, the money is with Faith?"

"But what if they've found Faith? It was Bridie who spoke. "What if they've found Faith and the money wasn't on her? What if they forced her to tell?

Maddy frowned. "You read that note, Bridie. Faith wanted to get Akuma where it hurts – right in the hip pocket. She wanted to undo what was done to her. This was personal. I don't think anything they did to her would make her tell. I also think," and here she paused for a moment to choose her words. "I think we should keep the money."

Bridie felt sick. Her head was swimming. Morally, she felt repulsed at the idea of keeping the money, but secretly, she was ashamed to admit, she too had been contemplating the idea of keeping the money. Her family had never been rich. She wasn't going to come by another windfall like this in a hurry. It could mean paying off most of her college debt or maybe even taking a trip overseas. The possibilities were endless.

"Do you really think we could pull it off?" she asked Maddy.

Camila stared open mouthed at Maddy and Bridie. "I can't believe you two are even entertaining the thought of doing this!"

"Why not, Camila?" Maddy stood suddenly. It's not like this belonged to some innocent person. This Akuma person deserves to never get their money back!"

"Look, I understand where you're coming from, Camila," said Bridie. I feel guilty at the thought of keeping it, but Maddy is right. We wouldn't be hurting anyone good." She looked appealingly at Camila. If we used it for good, wouldn't it be like Robin Hood stealing from the rich to give to the poor?"

"Yeah, but what about the danger factor? I can't believe it won't come back to bite us in the ass somehow."

"Well," said Bridie, scrambling for a solution, "What if we got new locks for the door and went home for a couple of weeks before school starts? We could leave the bag here, money and all, while we stay safe at home with our families. If after two weeks, there's no news of Faith, and the apartment hasn't been broken into, that would suggest that the trail has gone cold and we're in the clear."

"I like the sound of going home," Camila responded in a cold voice. "That's what I'm going to do. You two can do what you like with the money." She left in angry silence, shutting her bedroom door behind her.

By that evening, a locksmith had changed the locks and the three girls were on their way to their respective homes. Nobody had said much on departure. Everything had already been said in the frequent discussions they'd had throughout the day. The decision had been made. The duffle bag had been placed on the coffee table in the living room. The bait had been set. Now it was just a matter of time to see what happened next.

Bridie was glad to be away from the apartment and in the bosom of her own loving family, although her happiness was marred by the ugly secret she was keeping from her parents. Several times a day she would flip-flop in her resolve to keep the money. One minute she would determine to call Maddy and tell her the deal was off. The next minute she'd be dreaming of what she could buy with her share of the cash. It was on the eighth day, while she was setting the table for dinner, that she got a call from Maddy.

"I went back to the apartment today. The bag is still there."

"What? Maddy, are you crazy? That was a reckless thing to do, you could have been watched." Once again, Bridie's good sense, the good sense that had always served her well up until this point in her life, told her to wash her hands of the situation. "I'm starting to think this whole thing is a bad idea, Maddy. Let's take the bag to the police and forget about it."

"And how would that look? Taking the bag back a week after we got it? Wouldn't that implicate us in the whole Faith disappearance in some way? They'd want to know why we hung on to the money all this time. Do you want to explain that to the cops?"

"No, I guess not. But I wish I never listened to you in the first place." Bridie hung up, fighting back tears. She felt a mixture of confusion and resignation, as though she was getting swept along in a current that she was too weak to swim against. After the phone call, it became increasingly difficult to behave naturally around her family, and by the end of the visit, she was surprised to find that she was actually relieved to be going back to the apartment.

On the day, they were to go back, Bridie said an especially emotional farewell to her family. Her mother had stroked her hair and wiped her tears. "What's all this for?" She had said. "We'll be seeing you in November for Thanksgiving." Bridie hoped it was true.

The bus was crowded with commuters making the two-hour trip into the city from Bridie's hometown. She had arranged to meet Maddy and Camila at the bus depot before going to the apartment, but as the bus pulled into the bay, it was only Maddy who stood waiting with folded arms and an annoyed expression on her usually cheerful face.

"Hi!" She waved as she stepped off the bus. "Maddy! What's the matter? What's with the long face?"

"Camila just called. She said she isn't coming. She isn't coming back to the apartment at all – the coward. But, hey, that means more money for you and me, right?" Maddy's expression brightened at the thought.

"We won't even need another roommate to help with the rent now. Providing the bag is still there, of course."

Bridie found herself wishing fervently that she had Camila's courage. Nevertheless, she found herself following Maddy to their connecting bus, listening to her cheerful chatter. She was starting to wonder if she had ever really known Maddy, who seemed irritatingly comfortable with the whole situation. Maybe it wasn't a coincidence that she owned a padlock shim at all.

The duffle bag was still there. A fine layer of dust was proof that nobody had touched it, not even Maddy on her brief visit. The girls wandered through the apartment. Everything was neat, tidy and quiet, except for the McPherson's radio next door.

"Umm, it doesn't look like anyone was here," said Maddy returning from her bedroom. "I'd say this has all been a storm in a teacup. Faith has probably made it back home by now. The Akuma has no reason to suspect that the money is with us, so I think you and I just became two very lucky, and very rich, young ladies!"

Bridie watched Maddy dance around the apartment, whooping in delight. Could it be possible that they were safe? Could she allow herself to finally get excited about the money? The stress from the previous two weeks seemed to drain away in a matter of minutes. Maddy threw her arms around Bridie in an exuberant hug.

"So, what shall we do first, my little partner in crime?"

"Well... perhaps we should count it and divide it, and then...I think we should go SHOPPING!"

The girls screamed in jubilation, throwing any previous fears aside. What followed were weeks of unfettered spending. Gone from their minds were any thoughts of altruism. Maddy and Bridie were filled with a kind of reckless abandon. Like that of a person who finds themselves in the middle of a snake pit and it is just as far to retreat as it is to advance. And so, the girls made the most of it, being careful not to buy anything so expensive that they would have to explain where they got the money. Except for a few sharp-eyed girls at school who noticed an upgrade in their wardrobe and jewelry, nobody really seemed to notice anything unusual.

Camila knew what was going on, but she maintained a reserved silence on the subject. Bridie and Maddy rarely spoke with her anymore, except for the occasional "hello" in class. For Camila, it was an uncomfortable silence. There was nothing she would have liked to do more than going to the police. She still believed that they were in danger and wished fervently to be truly excised from the situation. But she said nothing, resorting instead to daily prayer for protection.

It was in October when things changed. The ground outside was carpeted in a blaze of orange, yellow and brown leaves, the trees reaching their black fingered branches up to a steel gray sky. Bridie loved the Fall, it was perfect weather for baking. It was a Saturday and she had spent the whole afternoon making homemade bread. The aroma wafted mouth-wateringly into the hall, making her neighbor's stomachs rumble in appreciation. Maddy was in the living room watching TV.

The phone rang. It was Camila.

"Are you watching the news?"

"No, what..."

"Switch it on, right now. Channel 6, news."

Wiping her flour-covered hands on a tea towel, Bridie hurried into the living room.

"Sorry," she said snatching the remote from Maddy's hand. This is an emergency."

"Hey! I was enjoying Ryan Gosling, here!"

"Sorry, but Camila called. There's something important on the news."

Bridie flicked the channel to six. She and Maddy watched as an aerial shot of a wooded parkland flickered onto the screen. Police were swarming the area, like ants. A coroner's van was parked nearby and what looked like a covered stretcher lay on the ground. In the corner of the screen was a picture of Faith's face, a smiling schoolgirl with her hair in a ponytail. Across the bottom of the screen read the words; BODY OF MISSING IOWA GIRL, FAITH BELLAMY FOUND.

"Oh, no." Bridie's voice was a whisper as her legs buckled under her and she sank to the floor.

"Turn it up!" Maddy barked, grabbing the remote back from Bridie. "They're saying something interesting."

"...the young woman from Barnaby's Creek was a student at Sanderson Community College and had been missing for over six months. There is evidence to suggest that she was groomed and seduced online by the sphinx-like Madam known only as Akuma or 'Demon', so named for her penchant for torturing her victims into submission before putting them on the street. Investigating police believe the young woman's death may be connected to her links with prostitution..."

At this point an image of a man and a woman, presumably Faith's parents, hollow-eyed and grief-stricken appeared on screen ready to take questions from reporters. Maddy clicked Mute and turned to Bridie who was shaking uncontrollably on the floor.

"O.K. Bridie, this is not the time to lose it. We must think this through logically. Stop crying, Bridie! That isn't going to help us at all!'

"It's over. We'll be next, now. You just watch."

"We don't know that for sure. It really all depends on how long ago, Faith died. Think, Bridie. If she was killed early on, then it means that this crazy cow, Akuma does not suspect us or she would have made her move by now. If Faith died recently, then there is still a chance that Akuma got the information about the money from her before she was killed.

Bridie glared at Maddy angrily. "And how do you propose to find out that little snippet of information, Maddy? Do we just sit here like sitting ducks and find out the hard way?"

"We have money, don't we? We just get away from here for a while. Take a room at a motel and lie low while the police investigate."

They were interrupted by a serendipitous knock on the door. A quick peep through the spy hole showed the calm exterior of Officer Blackthorne and her partner.

"It's the cops," hissed Maddy. Leave the talking to me. We've just found out about Faith, so it's alright to be a bit emotional." She opened the door. Officer Blackthorne said nothing, taking in the scene in a couple of seconds.

"Ah. I see you've heard the news?"

"Yes."

We need to ask you some more questions, Miss Fletcher," she said talking to Maddy, "and you too, Miss O'Keefe" she added, motioning to Bridie. "Is Miss, Ramirez here?"

"She doesn't live here anymore," sniffed Bridie.

"Very well." Blackthorne's sharp eyes took in the room, missing nothing. "That's a very nice and very big TV you have there. Did someone win the lottery?"

"It was my father's," said Maddy without skipping a beat. "He's upgrading."

"Lucky, you." Blackthorne sat on the sofa without being invited. Her companion, Officer Jane Pataki, remained standing. So far, she had never uttered a word in front of the girls. It was effectively intimidating.

Bridie ventured a question. "How did she die? They said on the television she was linked with prostitution. Has she been dead all this time?"

"We have reason to believe that Miss Bellamy has been on the run since the night your apartment was broken into. Forensics tell us that she died within the last 24 hours." Blackthorne's eyes met Bridie's. She was tortured. A jogger found her hanging in a tree."

Bridie felt her face flush hot and cold. Bile rose in her throat. It was all she could do to stop herself from throwing up. She could feel Maddy trembling beside her, although she was putting up a fierce attempt to hide her fear. It wouldn't be good to show their panic, but, thought Bridie, she could allow herself grief for Faith. Friend for one day, someone's daughter, someone's sister, hunted down, tormented and discarded like rubbish. Bridie let the tears flow hot and angry.

"Did they catch the one who did it?" Maddy's voice was husky with emotion. "The Akuma or devil people, or whatever they are?"

Here, Officer Pataki spoke for the first time. "The authorities know of Akuma by reputation and her impact in the crime world, but that is all. They believe it is a woman, but don't know for sure, possibly military trained and works alone. There is a link with prostitution but it doesn't seem to be her only motivation. Which begs the question, why did she feel it necessary to torture Miss Bellamy before her death? What did Miss Bellamy have or know?" Officer Pataki's eyes bored searchingly into first Maddy's and then Bridies eyes.

"Does a psycho need a reason to act like a psycho?" asked Maddy, scathingly. She folded her arms. "Thank you for telling us about Faith. Was there anything else you needed? Because we'd like to get back to our day if you don't mind."

Officer Blackthorne stood. "No, we were just here to inform you and to see if you'd had any contact with the victim in the last month or... if you'd noticed any suspicious activity in that time?" She raised one eyebrow.

Bridie roused herself. "No, no we haven't. It has been very quiet. We were with our families for a few weeks after the break-in and since then, nothing. Thank you for coming to tell us about Faith." She followed the officers to the door and watched them descend the stairs before closing the door behind her. She rounded on Maddy.

"Now what?"

"We don't panic, that's what." Maddy approached Bridie swiftly, placing her hands on her shoulders. "If we panic, we're liable to do something stupid. We've got to be calm and we've got to think smart."

"Akuma could be on her way to us as we speak. She could be here already, watching us!"

"If she is watching us and we start to act like there's something to panic about, she'll know that we know where the money is. Trust me on this, Bridie. We'll sit tight for another day, maybe two. We'll be careful. Then we'll get out of here."

"What about school? They're going to notice that we're missing."

"Bridie, we'll worry about that when the time comes – okay?"

Bridie said nothing. She didn't really have anything to say to Maddy anymore who she felt was to blame for the whole sorry mess. *But you had a choice,* a still small voice whispered on her shoulder. *You and only you are responsible for your actions.* "Oh, shut up," she muttered to herself as she went back to the kitchen.

The rest of the day dragged on, each second like a slow dripping tap. Maddy sat on the sofa like a poised cat, pretending to watch T.V. but ready to spring into action while Bridie who was listless, paced back and forth in the apartment, checking the window every ten minutes and testing the locks on the door.

As the day slipped into the evening they continued their vigil, taking it in turns to sleep while the other one watched, but there was no movement outside, no strange cars or strange sounds to give them cause to worry. When Bridie next opened her eyes, a blustery wind blew outside smacking fat raindrops against the window and Maddy was asleep sitting upright on a kitchen chair with her chin on her chest. The McPherson's radio spluttering into life as regular as clockwork jolted Maddy from her sleep.

"Must be eight o'clock," she said with a yawn.

Bridie laughed despite herself. She held her hand up against the cold autumn light. She was still alive. The events of the previous day seemed surreal.

It was decided between the two of them that living each day like the previous day was unsustainable. Nor would it go unnoticed to their neighbors or anyone watching, so they relaxed a little, even venturing out to the supermarket for supplies and meeting a few friends to play basketball at the park. All the while, counting the hours till the evening when they planned to make their move.

By nine o'clock they had packed a small bag each and taken a cab to the mall where they spent an hour or two shopping before catching a midnight screening of a movie. No one looked at them suspiciously or seemed to be following them. But when the movie was over and they filed out of the cinema, they found that it was almost deserted, with only a handful of cars in the carpark. The bus services were done for the night. The girls felt vulnerable and exposed. Thankfully, there was still one cab waiting at the taxi rank. The driver watched them under hooded eyes as they approached his window.

"Where to, ladies?"

"Do you know this address?" Maddy handed him a print out from the website of a previously selected motel about fifty miles away.

The cab driver leaned over and scrutinized the girls, taking in their appearance and clothes.

"That's a big fare. You sure you can pay?"

Maddy opened her wallet and peeled off two, one hundred dollar bills.

"Will this cover it?"

"Whaddya waiting for? Jump in."

The two girls sat quietly in the back seat while the driver tried in vain to draw them into some friendly conversation. After several attempts, he gave up and drove the rest of the way in silence, occasionally assessing them through his review mirror. They had all the signs of being runaways. Runaways from what? He didn't know. He didn't want to know. If he had a dollar for every suspect person he transported in his cab, he'd be a rich man. He glanced at the girls again in the mirror and memorized their general appearance, just in case he needed to know, and then he settled down for the long drive.

By the time the cab drew up to the motel it said 4: a.m. on the dashboard clock. The girls climbed out wearily, thanking the driver and telling him to keep the change. As the cab pulled away into the night, they trudged up to the reception window which was softly lit with a night light. Obviously, there was no one on duty at this hour. The girls shivered. It would mean sitting in the carpark until the first member of staff came on duty. They found a wooden bench out of the wind and huddled together, grateful for their warm coats. In that way, they dozed fitfully waiting for daylight.

The room was old-fashioned, its décor harking back to the eighties, shabby but comfortable and functional enough. It would have to do for now. After hot showers and some breakfast, they slept, long into the day. They planned to lie low for a few days before deciding what to do next. They had argued with the person at the desk when they wanted to pay with cash and she insisted they use a credit card. Now they had left another electronic trail for Akuma to follow. It would mean moving on. They spoke in hushed tones as they lay in their beds that night, while a wild storm thrashed the windows outside.

"How long are we doing to do this, Maddy? Sooner or later, someone is going to report us missing."

For the first time since the break-in, Maddy didn't have an answer. She was always so confident and assured. Bridie looked across the room at the dark form on the bed.

"Maddy?"

"I don't know anymore, Bridie. I just don't know."

She shifted on her bed and said no more. Bridie felt a chill of loneliness and fear. They were in way over their heads with this. They were truly alone.

The next day, they found their way to a second-hand car dealership, paying cash for a 2002 Ford Explorer. Having their own source of transport lifted their mood and gave them a greater sense of confidence. They wanted to be able to run at a moment's notice.

Their first stop was a beauty salon where they both had their long hair cropped short. Bridie had her blonde hair dyed auburn. Maddy had her dark hair bleached blonde. They watched each other's reflections in the salon mirrors and grinned. This might put some space between them and Akuma for a short while.

By noon, they were back at the motel. The Explorer's breaks squeaked as they pulled up in the carpark. Bridie pulled up the handbrake.

"I'll go to reception and pay for another night," Bridie told Maddy. "Can you make us a couple of sandwiches for lunch?"

"Sure." Maddy, slid out of the car, wrestling with several shopping bags while fumbling with the keys to their room. The wind was starting to get icy, whipping her hair back from her face and numbing her nose. She slid the fob over the electronic lock and the door popped open. She noticed the smell, the minute she entered the room. It was a delicate floral smell. It reminded her of passing a florist's shop. Fleeting, but pleasant.

Pleasant, yes, welcome, no. Maddy knew what was coming. In a frantic bid for freedom, she threw herself backward towards the door but it was too late. A black shroud fell over her face and she found herself trapped by a delicate arm, vicelike in strength. She fought wildly, choking as the feminine arm tightened like a Boa constrictor. Then a sharp sting in her arm. Her head began to swim.

"Relax, my dear," came a woman's voice in a soft monotone – then blackness.

It took fifteen minutes at the reception desk. Ten minutes to make the payment and five minutes to get away from the overly chatty receptionist. Her stomach rumbled as she made her way back to the motel room. She was starving and looking forward to some simple food after days of takeaway and room service. As she approached, she cursed Maddy under her breath. Why would she leave the door open in weather like this? It was freezing out here. From the open doorway, an empty plastic shopping bag was sucked out by the wind as though suddenly liberated from its contents. That's when Bridie saw the fob and car keys on the doorstep and her blood ran cold. Running, she threw herself through the door.

"Maddy? MADDY!"

She scanned the room quickly. The abandoned shopping bags were slumped on the ground. One dining chair lay on its side. Bridie ran through to the bathroom – nothing. Heart thumping, she turned, to look for Maddy outside, then froze in her tracks. Slowly, pivoting on the spot, she glanced back down at the dining table. There was something new on the table next to the complimentary tea and sugar sachets. A driver's license lay face down.

It felt like it was someone else's hand reaching down in slow motion to turn it over. But Bridie recognized her own nail polish and class ring as the hand picked up the license and turned over. It was an Iowa state license. A serious young woman's face stared back at her. Dark blonde hair and large gray eyes. Faith Bellamy was back from the dead.

Bridie dropped the license in horror staggering forward through the door and out to the car. Now she knew where Maddy was - Akuma.

Grabbing her purse, but leaving everything else behind, she ran to the car in a blind panic. Bridie jumped into the driver's seat and the engine burst into life, the tires screeching as she pulled out of the parking lot and headed back onto the freeway. Whimpering, she pushed the accelerator to the floor, weaving in and out of traffic, not knowing where she was going. Her gut instinct told her to go home. Maybe that's where she was headed?

As she drove she dialed the only other person she knew she could confide in. Camila's voice answered curious and concerned.

"Bridie?"

"Camila!" Bridie was sobbing. "She found us. Akuma found us. She has Maddy! I'm on the freeway and I don't know what to do! Can I come to your place?"

"No! Bridie, go to the police now! Maddy's life depends on it."

"But I'll be in so much trouble if I go to the police. I won't be able to face my family."

"You won't be able to face your family if you're dead. Go to the police. You can't do this on your own."

Suddenly, Bridie felt a kind of calm wash over her. It was what she had wanted to do from the start. The thought of handing it all over to someone bigger, smarter and stronger was so comforting.

"Hang on, Maddy," she prayed. "We're coming for you."

Bridie arrived in their hometown an hour and a half later. She had called on the way to report everything to Officers Blackthorne and Pataki who had ordered her to come to the precinct the minute she arrived in town. It was getting dark, downtown, but she still had difficulty finding a park close to the Police headquarters. Parking a couple of blocks away, she put a few coins in the parking meter and made her way up the street, nervously looking over her shoulder.

About fifty yards ahead on her side of the street, a man was approaching. He was powerfully built and wore a long black coat. His hair which was also long and dark covered his face. He kept his face down and his hands in his pockets, moving at a steady pace toward her. The hairs on the back of Bridie's neck stood on end. Her intuition told her that something was terribly wrong. Glancing across the street, she saw an elderly lady, tiny in stature, in a brown coat and a headscarf, trundling along at a snail's pace. Making a lightning decision, Bridie quickly trotted across the street, making a beeline for the old lady. There was safety in numbers.

On the other side of the road, Bridie felt a bit better, keeping a sharp eye on the man. He didn't look up but strode on steadily. For a moment, Bridie was confused. Maybe she was wrong. He didn't seem suspicious anymore. But her gut had sent a strong message to watch out.

The old lady was only a few yards away now. Her face was also directed at the ground as she carefully picked her way along the footpath. Bridie smiled, ready to say hello to her as they passed. As the old lady came up side by side with her, she glanced up. A pair of black, fathomless eyes met Bridie's. In a split second of regret, Bridie watched the old lady suddenly move with swift agility, throwing a black shroud over her head. She tried to scream, but she was held in an iron grip, cutting off her breath, threatening to crush her larynx.

"Struggling is futile," came the monotone voice, as Bridie was dragged down a side alley. Akuma slid a needle into Bridie's thigh. "Sweet dreams," she whispered.

When Bridie opened her eyes, she was in complete darkness. She had no concept of how much time had passed. Was it hours or days? It felt like days. Her tongue was fat and dry in her mouth and felt alien, like it didn't belong there. She tried to produce some saliva to lubricate her tongue but it was stuck fast. A moan bubbled up inside her unable to escape. Breathing through her nose, she attempted to calm herself. Remembering Maddy's approach to most crisis'. What was it she said? *If we panic we're liable to do something stupid.* Well, she'd already done that. Now she had to keep her wits about her if she wanted any hope of escaping.

She listened to the room. She could hear dripping pipes. Very faint in the distance she could hear cars, but too far away to be of any help. It was like an ice box. The stone or cement floor penetrated cold through her jeans. And there was a slight smell of something rotten. "I'm in a basement of some kind," she thought.

She went to stand up. Her head throbbed at the movement making her pause while the pain settled. Her stomach growled. She could have been here for days for all she knew. Slowly, she began a painstaking exploration of the room with her hands, carefully sliding them over every inch of the walls which were mostly bare. Suddenly, her fingers fluttered over the end of an exposed pipe. It was wet! The source of the dripping sound! Not waiting or caring to find out if it was safe to drink, Bridie shoved her mouth up to the pipe allowing the delicious liquid to hydrate her swollen tongue. Slowly, she was able to open her mouth enough to take a drink.

Revived somewhat, Bridie continued her search, inching along the perimeter of the room. Suddenly, she bumped her foot into something heavy. Leaning down, her hand brushed against something soft. Hair! She pulled back her hand in horror. Was it an animal? In her panic, the heavy something slid down the wall and fell with a *whump*. A loud gasping moan cut the silence like a knife. It was a person! Maddy, maybe injured?

Bridie reached down grasping wildly in the dark. Her hands met with something cold. A face. The eyes closed – the mouth open.

"Maddy? Can you hear me? It's me! Wake up!"

As her hands explored the body, the face, the neck, the shoulders, and arms, she suddenly found where there should have been an elbow a wet stump. Her fingers sank into the wet mess and slid off a nub of bone. Suddenly the rotten smell made sense. It was a corpse.

Bridie started to gag. Common sense cast aside. She threw herself wildly across the room, frantic to find a door or a light switch, banging on the walls, screaming at the top of her lungs. All at once the room was flooded with light from a window in the door, rendering her temporarily blind. A voice came crackling over an intercom. The same monotone she had heard under the black shroud.

"Ah, I see you are awake."

The first image that materialized as Bridie's eyes adjusted to the light was that of Maddy's brutalized body lying open-mouthed on the other side of the room. Bridie, sobbed softly, impotent rage bubbling up inside her at the killer on the other side of the door.

"I am about to open the door. Please move to the other side of the room and do not attempt to escape. I have a gun you see, and I'd rather not use it yet," she said in a soft Japanese accent. "Your friend found out the hard way."

Bridie complied. Her mind racing for ways to escape. The door opened. A woman of petite stature dressed in an elegant pantsuit stood silhouetted against the light at the bottom of a staircase. Bridie stared at her with undisguised hatred.

"What do you want from me?" she snarled.

"All kinds of things." Akuma laughed mirthlessly. "But firstly, I would like my money. Faith was very naughty to have given it to you."

"It's back at our apartment. Go and get it. I don't care. We spent some, but I can get the rest for you. Just let me go, please?"

"Oh, no. That would be no fun at all." She pointed the gun at Bridie, stepping into the basement room so that she could pass by. "After you," she said, indicating up the stairs.

Bridie obeyed, climbing the steep stairs. At the top, she found herself in a laboratory with an examination table of sorts in the center, the kind you might find in a doctor's surgery, only this one sported leather straps and shackles. Bridie stopped short, terror coursing through her veins. She began to cry again, this time in humiliation as she felt a warm trickle of urine running down her leg. How would she ever be able to endure what was coming?

"Oh, dear. I thought you would have been braver than this. It's Bridie, isn't it? Your friend was very stoic, I must say. Now lie down, there's a good girl."

Bridie didn't move. She *couldn't* move. Her feet felt glued to the floor. She felt the cold steel of the gun against her back.

"I said lie down."

Bridie lay down on the table, praying silently. Fast as a snake, Akuma was beside her, sinking another syringe into her arm. Bridie felt herself go limp expecting to go to sleep. *At least I'll be asleep when she does it*, she thought gratefully. But as the minutes ticked by, her mind remained alert. Akuma, busied herself, strapping Bridie into the restraints, then smiled knowingly at Bridie, leaning close to her face.

"Yes," she murmured thickly. "You'll be able to feel everything."

She pulled a nearby trolley close covered in shining instruments. Bridie could smell disinfectant as Akuma picked up what looked like a heavy set of pliers and brandished them in front of her face.

"I don't want to disfigure you too badly. You won't get many customers if I do that." she paused to pull on some gloves. "But I do want to teach you to be obedient, my dear."

With that, Akuma picked up a circlet of plastic which Bridie recognized immediately as a mouth prop used by dentists to hold their patient's mouths open. She began to shriek and struggle wildly as Akuma fitted the prop into her mouth, but the shrieking and struggling were all in her mind. Her body remained as limp as a blanket. Akuma picked up the pliers again.

"Now if you'll just hold still."

Bridie felt the cold steel on her lips. She braced herself as she felt the pliers clasp one of her molars in a vice-like grip. Akuma grunted with effort, wrenching Bridie's tooth from her jaw in a savage twist. Bridie's brain exploded in shuddering, psychedelic agony. Again, and again the pain came in torturous waves. Then as she felt herself beginning to black out, there was a sudden loud bang in the next room and the door to the lab was knocked off its hinges and a SWAT team appeared in the doorway, bellowing commands with their weapons drawn.

"GET YOUR HANDS IN THE AIR AND GET ON THE GROUND, NOW!"

The team poured into the tiny lab. Akuma drew her gun and let off a volley of shots at the officers. They returned fire riddling her body with bullets and sending her flying backward down the stairs where she lay crumpled and lifeless at the basement door.

Bridie drifted in and out of consciousness. Officer Blackthorne was by her side and so was Camila. What was Camila doing here? She was vaguely aware of sirens and the inside of an ambulance and Camila sitting by her side crying and holding her hand.

Bridie's voice was hoarse. "Camila, Maddy's dead. She's dead."

"I know. I'm so sorry. I should have gone to the police earlier. I was too late!"

"No, I'm the one who's sorry. I should have listened to you."

But then the morphine had started to kick in and she'd drifted blissfully on a cloud wanting to forget everything for a while. She wanted to enjoy it while it lasted.

There would be plenty of time later to face the music.

CUT AND RUN

ROBERT BRISCOE

Paul wanted out.

He did love Kate, at least in the beginning. She had a cute face and a voluptuous body which began to lose the battle with gravity over the years. Her once cheerful personality faded along with her looks over time. She once greeted him at the door with a bright smile and a hug. But now, she always looked angry. Her eyes would shift from left to right and there was a distant quality about her.

Paul met her through a Christian dating service. He had written out exactly what he wanted in a woman and placed the ad. Within a week, he had arranged a date with Kate and they were married eight months later.

He looked at some pictures of his mother in her youthful prime and couldn't help but notice how much Kate looked like her. They had identical world-views as well, being devoutly religious, at least with their words. With their deeds, well, that had always been another story for his mother as well as his wife.

"You need to stop hanging out with the boys so much," Kate said as Paul headed out the door. "You know, we hardly ever do anything together anymore."

"Fine," Paul sighed. "I'll stay. Let's go out. We can go to that new Korean place."

"No, no," Kate said. "You do your thing."

She said that as if she were a martyr. But Paul knew about Kate. He knew about Kate's secrets just like he knew his mother's.

She had been cheating on him. He had the proof now.

He had hired a private detective that tailed her around for a few weeks. He confirmed Paul's suspicions and delivered an envelope with the "proof."

"You were right," the private detective sighed. "But like I said in the beginning, if you suspect it, it is already true so you can save yourself the money."

Paul thanked the man although he really didn't know why. He had been brought up to be so polite. He had the envelope for over a week now. He couldn't bring himself to open the package yet. He didn't want to know all of the details yet, like the identity of the men or where they held their trysts.

His mother did the same thing to his father. Cheated on him with his best friend. His Dad stayed in the marriage until Paul reached adulthood. Paul liked to think that his father stayed for his sake. He appreciated that about his Dad.

But he couldn't be like him.

Faithful and committed but living a lie.

He could only feel an abstract form of sympathy for his father. His Dad had always been distant and quiet, as if he had his own secrets.

"Never trust anyone," his father said to him in a very quiet voice one day when they were out fishing. "Don't trust anyone. Just cut and run."

But Paul felt that sometimes even his own father didn't trust him. So he kept secrets when he was a kid.

And he continued to do things in secret, just like his parents.

Courtney side-stepped her way through the hallway, sliding past people that she hardly ever saw outside their cubicle. They stuffed their already obese faces with cake as they milled around a long center table in the middle of the hall.

An office potluck filled with congealed macaroni and cheese, seven-layer salads, potato chips and slices of cold cuts from a person too lazy to cook.

There were large bottles of Hawaiian Punch, Dr. Pepper and Pepsi with Styrofoam cups on the side. For dessert, someone made a 7-Up cake while another brought a box of donuts.

"You have to try my carrot cake, Courtney," Gwen said, holding a plastic plate out for her.

"Looks good," Courtney said, continuing down the hallway. "I've gone paleo though."

It all made Courtney's stomach uneasy. She hated the food of office parties. She hated the office. Period.

"It is just way too noisy out there," Courtney said, poking her head in Dan's office. "Do you mind if I use the phone in here."

"No worries," Dan said, looking out his office window at the revelry taking place in the main hallway.

"My cell phone is out," Courtney shook her head, waving her device in the air.

She looked over at Dan and felt a bit sorry for him. The soft-spoken Chinese man had been with the software company for over ten years now but most people kept him at arm's length.

Courtney plopped down on his desk chair. No pictures of family. No pictures of friends. Dan was probably the only person in the office that she wasn't Facebook friends with as he had no other social media profile other than a few lines on LinkedIn.

No one knew anything about him. The quiet and polite guy that kept to himself.

He closed the door and looked over at Courtney.

"I've been wanting to ask you something," he said.

"What?"

She saw his eyes immediately drop to the floor as he shuffled his feet like a shy junior high school student.

"Dan?"

"Nothing," he said, smiling to himself. "Never mind. I should be going." He walked over to the window and took his folded coat off the ledge.

"You sure?" Courtney asked. "You looked like you had something important on your mind."

"It wasn't," Dan said. "I just lost my train of thought, that's all. If I remember it, I'll just e-mail you."

"I do it all the time," Courtney said.

"Do what?"

"Lose my train of thought. Like the typical ditzy blonde. Like just now I forgot what I was going to tell my boyfriend."

"You have a boyfriend?" Dan's face betrayed surprise and disappointment.

"Yeah."

"I'm heading out," Dan picked up his umbrella off the floor, eyes now peeled to the ground as if in mourning. "Have a nice weekend, Courtney."

"Thank you," Courtney cradled the receiver to her ear. "You do the same."

Dan walked out of the office, looking back at Courtney, the attraction in his face all too obvious.

Courtney felt bad. She knew that the majority of the programmers in the office had crushes on her. They were all too shy or awkward to even approach her. She knew that they put her on a pedestal like the nerds did on that show with Kaley Cuoco. In fact, she facially resembled Cuoco and that had not been a week that went by when someone randomly mentioned that to her.

She watched through the window as Dan maneuvered his way through the crowd. No one seemed to acknowledge or notice him. She had a "type" and Dan did not fit her criteria. She liked her men virile. Confident.

And smart.

Like Paul Spence.

She didn't know why she fell for him so hard. He made her feel like a 7th grader, like a teenybopper whose chest filled with butterflies whenever her crush walked by in the hallway.

Smiling to herself, she dialed and waited.

"Yeah?" the voice on the other end sounded gruff.

"What do you mean, 'yeah'?" Courtney said. "Is that any way to answer the damn phone?"

"I'm sorry," Paul said. "I tried calling you but your cell phone keeps dropping dead."

"Yeah, well, let's not take that as an omen," Courtney said. "Did you do the deed? Because if you haven't I'll do it myself. She needs to know."

"Don't do that," Paul said. "I don't want you to ever meet her."

"That doesn't answer my question."

"Okay. Yeah, I told her."

"You did?" Courtney stood up from the chair, feeling so happy that she could jump through the roof. "I can't believe it. Really? What did she say?"

"Well, she didn't get as upset as I thought she would," Paul said. "Maybe that's encouraging."

"I don't believe you," Courtney said. "You didn't tell her, did you? I'll fucking tell her myself."

"Easy, baby. Easy. I did tell her. I laid out all the terms. Even gave her a written offer which she

could take to her attorney. She was about to rip it up. Then I showed her the photos. Photos of her with her beau. She called her lawyer and he told her to agree to the terms."

Courtney sat back down with a smile on her face. "Christmas just came early. That is fucking awesome. These folks are about to bounce out of here. I'll come straight over, okay? We have to celebrate."

"Russ and I are getting ready to watch the fight," Paul said. "I'll come there and pick you up, okay? You're going to have an empty office, right?"

"Ooooh. I like where you're going with that. I love you."

"Love you too," Paul said. "Bye."

Paul clicked off his cell and looked over at Russ. His best friend downed another can of beer, chugging it like a baby on a bottle.

"Trouble in paradise?" Russ asked before belching. Everything about the man represented crudeness and college-aged rebellion. He had pictures of vintage Playboy centerfolds on his wall mixed in with autographs of football players from their beloved San Francisco 49ers. That may have been part of his appeal to Paul and his other childhood friends. They all still managed to gather around every six months or so in his shitbox of an apartment. To let themselves go for one evening of entertainment with a man who refused to grow up.

"The shit I get myself into," Paul said, looking at his Smartphone at a selfie picture of Courtney wearing only a bra.

"Just gotta cut yourself loose," Russ said, squeezing the empty beer can like an accordion before stuffing his face with a slice of pizza.

"I wish I had it like you," Paul said. "You got it simple, Playboy. A one bedroom apartment that overlooks the bay. A flat screen TV. A couch. A bed. What else do you need?"

"The grass ain't always greener on the other side," Russ tucked his head into his chest and belched again, his chin piling into a rippled series of fat folds. "You have what I want. A beautiful wife and a blonde mistress that is just hot as fuck."

"I don't now where the marriage went wrong," Paul said. "And I thought marriage 2.0 was just shacking up with someone. But Courtney wants me to divorce Kate and marry her. Like I'd want to go through what I went through with Kate all over again."

"What are you going to do?"

"I can't leave Kate," Paul said, more to himself than to Russ. "That would crush her. Crush her family. Crush my family."

"Then you have no choice but to cut your little office girl loose. Go back home to the wifey and stay secure with her family fortune. Shit, man, where do I sign up?"

"I don't know how I can get rid of this one," Paul said. "You know, they act like they don't want anything serious but it's all just a ruse. It is all damn serious. They want what they can't have."

"Of course," Russ said. "From an objective point of view, you're playing with fire. So I would advise you to just disappear from her life. That's how my old man used to ditch his girlfriends. Just cut them off. But today, with social media and whatnot she will track your ass down and tell your wife and do whatever the hell it takes to shame you. Who knows what she has on you? Maybe she recorded a video and will tag you on Facebook if you act up. This social media is a way to hold people hostage in situations like this."

Paul nodded his head, taking a slice of pizza from the carton on the table. He took a bite, wincing at the sour taste of the now stale sauce on hard bread.

"What would your old man do if he were in my situation?"

"He would make it seem as if breaking up was her idea."

"How would he do that?"

"You gotta play the role of the suffocating geek," Russ said. "You know, give her flowers, act overly nice, fawn over her. Call her on the phone constantly. Suffocate the shit out of her. She'll drop your ass."

"I think that will only make things worse."

"Only if you make it romantic. You have to make it seem needy. Do whatever it takes to make yourself repulsive. Write her love letters. Read it to her and cry."

"Shit," Paul laughed. "I can't do that. I was really bad in high school drama and she'd see right through me. I'm too nice to her as it is. I asked what it was that she saw in me and she said she liked me because I was nice. Not because I had money or a deep voice or blue eyes. Just that I was nice."

"Bullshit," Russ laughed. "Never take what a woman says at face value. And nice guys don't cheat on their wives. Tell her that."

"Judge away, Playboy," Paul said. "You're single. You don't know what it's like."

"You know I'm just joshing you," Russ said. "My dad cheated on my mom. I didn't judge him. My mom was a bitch and they fought constantly. I don't blame him. But when she found out about my Pop's affairs, she changed. Mellowed out a bit. So maybe it was good for both of them."

"This can't really end well," Paul said. "I just have to break it off and hope that time heals the wounds."

"Look, man," Russ got up from the sofa and stretched. "Millions of men have tried to have mistresses on the side. All have failed. Either the mistress holds them ransom or the wife finds out somehow. Any affair, long term, will come to the light of day."

Paul stood up without saying a word and headed to the door. He had about a half-hour drive to Courtney's office.

"And here I thought you could give me advice," Paul said. "I'll see you on the good side."

"You're not staying to watch the fight?" Russ blocked his path. "Tony and Efren were totally down to see you."

"I have a mistress to attend to," Paul stepped aside and opened the door.

"So now I have a sausage party to look forward to. See? I was never the ladies' man you are and never will be."

"It isn't what it's cracked up to be," Paul said.

Paul took the steps rather than the elevator up to the fifth floor of Courtney's office. This allowed him to slide in past the receptionist and into the side hallway.

He wanted no witnesses. He had been good about that.

Courtney knew the drill and liked all of the cloak and dagger moves they had to make. They would check into a hotel under an assumed name and they would meet there in disguises. Other times they would go to a bar and pretend not to know each other. They would then eyeball each other from across the room and role play. Sometimes she would be a Russian spy. Sometimes he would be a British high-roller.

He did the same routine with all of the women he had affairs with and they all loved it. Paul thought about them all, sometimes daydreaming about the women. His mind soon becoming a kaleidoscope of under-lit hotel rooms, whispered phone calls and naked bodies. The memories both excited and repulsed him.

Paul opened the door and the dimly lit hallway remind him of the many times he sneaked into a hotel room after hours, meeting the mistress of the month.

"Courtney?" Paul called out as he neither heard nor saw any signs of life in the office.

"Paul?" Courtney poked her head out of the back office and ran over to greet him.

She leaped onto him like a military wife greeting her husband in one of those viral videos. Paul's heart softened. He could not let this go. The attention, the softness of her perky breasts pressed up against him. The greedy way she kissed him, the sleepy smile she gave him after he climaxed inside her.

Kate never made him feel like that. At least that is what he told himself.

"Not here," Paul said, whisking her into the back office.

"No one is here," Courtney said. "Just the janitor."

"And they know everything," Paul said, closing the door behind himself.

"Please tell me we can go through with it now," she said, wrapping her arms around him and once again pressing her breasts up against him.

"Go through with what?" Paul said with a devilish grin.

"You know what," Courtney pulled back. "I don't want us to keep running around like we're fugitives anymore."

"We're fugitives of love," Paul said, kissing her neck until hearing a thump from outside the office door. "The hell was that?"

"The janitor. Duh. Maybe a rat.

Paul looked out of the office window and saw the Asian woman push the vacuum across the carpet, buds from her Ipod in both of her ears.

He turned off the light in the office and pulled down the window blinds.

"What are you doing?"

"Lock the door," Paul said.

"Why?"

"I don't want the janitor coming in. Do you want to give her a free show?"

"I thought we were done sneaking around. I don't care who knows about us now. Or who watches. It would be kind of a turn on actually."

Courtney took Paul's hand and rubbed it against her crotch, sighing hard.

"I just want our privacy," he said, closing his eyes as if that would fight off his excitement. Courtney would take him places sexually that Kate never would. Make him do things that he would never do with his wife.

"Fine," Courtney pushed him away with some playfulness. She walked over to the desk drawer, took out a keychain and locked the door. "If you want to be shy and modest who am I to argue? You be the shy nerd. I'll play the seductress."

"We can't be caught until everything goes through," Paul said, not playing along. "So now we have to be extra careful."

"Okay," Courtney threw up her hands. "Now for the details. How soon is this going to happen?"

"Soon."

"Is she going to file first or you?"

"She will."

"Then we'll get married immediately after?"

"Yeah, yeah," Paul ran his hands through his hair before peeking back through the window. No janitor in sight. "We just have to let the courts do their thing."

"I know," Courtney said. "But we can plan our honeymoon now. I was thinking that we could go to the Caribbean but now I'm leaning toward Montreal. Or Italy. I was looking on-line and I can't decide. I want to take a gondola ride. I want to lay on the beach. I want to go to an art museum, then take a hike up someplace remote, then maybe-"

"You're all over the map," Paul laughed. "But let's make sure that Kate fills her end of the bargain first."

"You have doubts?" Courtney asked.

"She's a flaky bitch," Paul shook his head. "One flaky ass bitch. She says one thing one day and the next day it is something else."

"So she's going to play games? That's what she's going to do, right? Stall it out forever and then make us wait forever."

"We'll have to wait and see."

Courtney began to pace back and forth. She looked up at him, like a child, and stomped her feet.

Paul knew that he had that kind of control over her. He would make her feel like a little kid, a little girl that never got enough of her father's attention. He had a way of controlling the conversation with her that made her feel helpless and she loved him for it.

"That bitch," she hissed. "That fucking bitch."

Paul grabbed her by the arm and pulled her against his chest. "You just don't know her," he said. "This has been a long time coming. A long time. She may stall this out, yeah. Just to spite me. That is how rich people are. She said she would go through with it but I know now that she's plotting. She won't go away without trying to injure me emotionally somehow. Then she may come after you."

"What are you saying?" Courtney pulled away from his grasp, staring daggers into his eyes. Her lips locked tightly over her teeth and a vein throbbed in the middle of her forehead.

"I'm saying we have to lay low for awhile," Paul said. "She finds out that I've left her for another woman then she's going to get pissed. I called her out on her bullshit. She cheated on me. I have that over her. But if she found out that I was cheating on her, that would put a whole new paint job on things."

"I see."

"See if I stick around," Paul said. "I'll convince her that this was all her idea. That it was her decision all along and that this separation is for the best."

Courtney didn't say anything. She just stared. "So you have no timetable?"

"I don't think it will happen right away," Paul said. "I don't know. A few weeks. We have to let her ease into it. Make it her play, not mine."

"You sound more interested in her feelings than mine," Courtney said. "You just told me her attorney advised her to go through with it. You told me she made you miserable. I make you happy. What is the problem?"

"There isn't one," Paul stepped closer until they were chest to chest again. He kissed her cheek and forehead. "Now let's go celebrate. Just the two of us."

"Celebrate what?"

"Us."

"Let me make a call first," Courtney said walking back over to the desk phone.

Paul sighed and turned his back to his mistress. He walked over to the side window and remembered his own days as a cubicle monkey. He spent more time staring out the window and dreaming, fantasizing about the new secretary or sales girl that came into his office. Then he met Kate who became his benefactor of sorts. He could pursue his dream of teaching art and seducing young students in night classes.

Like Courtney.

"Hello?" Courtney said. "Kate?

Paul sprinted over and grabbed the phone out of Courtney's hand, slamming it back on the desk. "The fuck are you doing?"

"Taking the bull by the horn," Courtney said. "I'm going to let her know, Paul. You're divorcing her and marrying me. I'm calling her and letting her know. Don't even try and stop me."

Paul grabbed her by both arms and shook her.

"Didn't you hear what I said?" he screamed. "If you do that I have nothing on her. The affair she is having is negated and I can't get anything in the deal."

"Is that all you care about? The money?"

"No."

"This is about love, right?" Courtney said. "Our love. And I'm making things right."

Courtney pushed him away, sat down in front of the phone and began dialing again.

He realized then that what made Courtney so irresistible to him now became intolerable. He could make her feel like a little girl, but lately, she would be able to flip the script on him.

She could make him feel helpless, like a little boy.

She would scold him, playfully, treating him like his mother used to treat him.

Like someone who had no power.

"Put the phone down, Courtney."

"Shut the fuck up, Paul," she said, waving him away as if he were a gnat. "You're just like my Dad. Spineless."

Her snarky comment gave him a flashback of a time when his mother chastised him for doing something that he had forgotten about. All he remembered were the words she said. Words that echoed in his brain for years.

You're going to be just like your father. I can't depend on you. You'll be late. You'll forget. You'll let me down.

"Put the fucking phone down."

"Paul. Shut. The. Fuck. Up," Courtney turned her back to him.

Time to stop obeying mother.

He reached over and wrapped the phone cord around Courtney's throat.

"Paul!" she reached back, her fingernails digging into his neck until he squeezed harder.

He glanced behind himself even though he knew they were alone and the blinds were shut. Then he looked to the ceiling as if God were watching.

This can't be happening. I can't be killing her. Can I?

He closed his eyes and squeezed. Waiting and waiting. Harder and harder. His heart began pounding harder in his chest as she fought for her breath.

Paul expected some kind of crisis of conscience, some kind of impediment or moral barrier for him to fight past. He never thought that he could be capable of such a thing and had contempt for people who commit murder.

That voice, that invisible arm from above that he expected to stop him never came.

He released his grip from the cord and used his hands instead, pressing into the sides of her neck. After what seemed like a few minutes, she dropped to the floor, lifeless.

Paul stood frozen in place, waiting for some epiphanic realization to take place, some voice from above to condemn him. Paul knew that this was one of those moments that would ruin him for life, but now, at the present time, it held very little meaning. The meaning would come after, in hindsight, and he knew he would have many dark nights of the soul.

He looked down and she moved her neck once as if she were trying to shake her head 'no'. Her eyes remained shut. Paul noted how she made no noise, no death rattle, no final gasp for breath. What was once the happiest soul he had ever met now laid in front of him like a broken rag doll.

Paul looked over at the side window and saw a cloud shadow moving across the full moon.

"Hello?" Paul heard his wife's voice on the other end of the phone. "Hello?"

Paul picked the receiver up from the ground and placed it back onto the cradle, hanging up on his wife. He took a deep breath, closed his eyes and started to count. By the time he reached the count of twenty, he knew what he had to do.

Run.

Paul rushed to the door and found it locked.

"Shit," he said, walking back over to Courtney's purse on the desk and taking out her set of keys. He inserted the key, twisted and it broke in half inside the keyhole. "Shit!"

Paul tried in vain to pull out the broken key. Too far inside, he panicked as he felt as if the God's above were locking him in.

He took a few steps over to the hallway window and opened the blinds.

No housekeeper in sight. He looked for a latch to open the window up but found none. Desperate, he picked up the ergonomic conference chair from behind the desk and threw it at the glass.

It simply bounced off.

He tried again to no avail, slamming the chair again and again before breaking off one of the wheels.

Frustrated, he tried the door again. Turning the knob over and over before messing with the broken keyhole again.

No progress.

"Gotta be a way out this shit box," Paul muttered to himself. He walked over to the side window and raised it open. He looked down and got dizzy at the prospect of jumping out. They were five stories up.

Think. Think. Think.

Paul tried to occupy his mind solely with thoughts of an escape. He could feel the danger in thinking about what he had just done, sensing that if he did that it would only lead to anxiety and inaction. He had to think forward, control the things he had control over.

Hide the body.

His adrenaline finally started to subside as he looked back down at the dead body of Courtney. His mind started to race and entered survival mode. How could he get away with this? He had to wipe down the whole damn office of his fingerprints. Then he had to clear his number from Courtney's cell phone but the authorities would be able to trace her calls anyway.

Fuck! Too much to think about!

Paul took off his shirt and began wiping down the doorknob, the desk phone, and the chair. Then he randomly wiped down everything else as he could not remember what he touched and what he didn't.

He took out Courtney's cell phone from her purse, his shirt covering his hands, and began navigating through her settings. He deleted his phone number from her address until the phone died from the depleted battery.

Shit!

He looked down at her body again.

All of this trouble for a piece of ass.

Feeling angrier now, he picked up Courtney by her shoulders and dragged her over to the side window.

He stopped short of shoving her through the window, instead gauging how she easily she could fit through.

Splat! No witnesses.

But someone would eventually walk by and make the call. The police and fire department would come and here he would be in her office, locked in.

Try explaining that.

The interrogations would come fast and furious. They would wear him down through attrition.

No, there had to be a better way.

For now, he had to get her out of his sight.

He picked up Courtney back up and pulled her next to the storage closet. Opening the door, he stood her up to make her fit inside then shut the door behind her, her body curling up like an accordion.

Paul took out his cell phone and dialed Russ.

"Wassup," Russ said after only two rings.

"I need a favor," Paul said. "Big time."

"What is it?"

"I need your help. My girl is passed out drunk. Now she's locked me in her office. She works at NextCom. Do you know where that's at?"

"Locked you in her office," Russ said laughing. "Dude, you are a hot mess. You hear me? A hot mess."

"Yeah, yeah," Paul said. "Look, man, the door is stuck."

"Isn't there anyone who can let you out?"

"If there was someone I wouldn't be calling you, would I?"

"Chill, man."

"There's no one here. I don't want to call the fire department. Now the building is going to be closed through the weekend."

"The fight is about to start, man," Russ said, his speech starting to slur from the effects of drinking a six-pack and more. "I'll come after the fight."

"Seriously, dude. I'll text you the address. Nextcom building. Fifth floor. Got it?"

"Alright, man," Russ said, his voice fading out in disinterest.

He heard Russ click the off button and he texted the address over to him.

Thanks, man. As soon as you can, owe u big time.

Feeling claustrophobic, Paul rushed toward the door, pulling, twisting and tugging as hard as he could. The door wouldn't move.

Feeling his cell phone buzz in his pocket, he picked it up immediately.

"Russ?"

"Super good fight, man," Russ said. "You don't know what you're missing."

"I'm missing out because I'm locked in a damn office," Paul said. "How much longer?"

"I don't know. It looks like the type of fight that will go the distance. I can't just leave the boys here. They're pissed because you didn't come."

"Come on, man, I'm stuck here."

"Whoa!" Russ said on the other end. Paul could hear the sounds of Tony and Efren whooping. "Holy shit-what a shot!"

The line went dead again.

"Russ? Russ?"

A part of him knew he was now different from his friends. He felt the same but could no longer be one of the guys enjoying a boxing match over pizza and beer. They didn't know how lucky they were.

Paul was no longer one of the guys.

He killed a woman. He was a murderer.

Then he heard shuffling behind the door of the storage closet.

Can't be.

Courtney.

He moved over on the balls of his feet and pressed his ear against the door. Then with a forceful resolve, he opened it up and Courtney fell down at his feet.

Looking up at him as if trying to focus her eyes. "Why?" she wheezed before coughing.

Paul panicked, his heart began to race. He must have just choked her out and not killed her.

"I fucking loved you," Courtney began to move to get up, rolling up on her forearms. She coughed hard and grabbed at his pant leg.

He knelt down next to her, listening as she tried to say something else. Her voice was rough, barely more than a whisper. She looked up at her tormentor, blinking her eyes hard. Her nose bled and she had a red streak above her mouth. It gave her face the look of a drug-addled Anna Nicole Smith when she did herself up in clown make-up.

"I'm sorry," he said.

"You fucker," she wheezed. "You dumb shit."

Paul picked her up off the ground and led her to the couch, sitting her down. He sat next to her, not knowing whether to place his arm around her or give her space.

"I'm going to tell your wife," she said, her voice becoming clearer by the second. "I'm going to ruin you. I'll ruin everything about you. Your marriage. Your family. Your job. Everyone will know. Everyone will-"

Paul clamped his hand on Courtney's mouth. He squeezed and squeezed. This time, his desire was made clear in his head.

This bitch had to die.

She clawed at his face and he could feel her nails dig deep into his skin. She bit down on his hands, making animal sounds as she tried to escape his choke.

But he didn't care. She had to-

"Shut up!"

Paul twisted her head with such force that he could hear her the tiny bones in her neck crack.

No longer hesitating, Paul dragged her by the hair back to the closet and slammed the door shut.

Exasperated, he picked the chair up and placed it upright on the ground. The wheel wobbled as he placed at back at the desk and then he caught a glimpse of the woman in the window across the way.

A Chinese woman, maybe in her early 50s with her hair up in a braid. She pushed a vacuum back and forth across the carpet. The same woman that had been outside the hallway window.

It made sense. The two office towers were joined together by one interconnecting hallway.

Maybe he could get her to come back over and let him out?

"Hey!" Paul screamed as he opened the window. He began waving his arms and doing jumping jacks but the woman wouldn't look in his direction.

Desperate, he took a stapler from the desk and toss at the window across the way.

The shattering glass startled the woman and she looked over at Paul with her mouth open.

"Hi!" Paul bellowed. "So sorry. So sorry. I'm locked in here. I was hoping you could come over and unlock the door."

The woman froze in place at the window. She moved out of Paul's line of vision for a beat then returned with a cell phone in her hand.

"Come on," he said. "Don't do that. I'm locked in here. Do you understand?"

He saw the lady move toward the window as if to get a better look at him.

"I'm locked in! Locked in!"

She then backed out of his line of vision again, talking on the phone.

"Shit," Paul said. He began putting things back into place around the office; taking the phone off the floor, closing the windows and then straightening out the sofa.

He looked back into the storage closet at the body of Courtney.

No coming back to life this time.

Paul didn't hear any sirens but when he looked out the window again he saw the Chinese woman conferring with two police officers. Paul waved at one of the cops who nodded his head and then left the room.

After a few minutes, Paul could hear shuffling outside the office door.

"Sir?" a stern voice outside the door said. "Can you open up please?"

"That's the thing officers," Paul said. "I can't. I've been locked in here."

"Don't you have the key?"

"The key broke in the lock," Paul said.

He saw the door knob start to jiggle.

"We can't open it from outside," one of the officers said.

"Maybe the housekeeper has the key?" Paul said but he didn't think the officers were listening.

"I don't want to call the fire department for this shit," Paul heard one of the policemen say. "Sir, just stand back a second!"

Paul moved a few feet away from the door. Next, he heard a large thump at the door then another. Finally, the police officers slammed their shoulders through the door, knocking it off its hinges.

"Thanks so much," Paul said. "Thought I'd be here all night."

"Why didn't you call us?"

There were two officers at the door. They looked liked twins save for the fact that one had black hair and the other was bald. They were both short, under five-foot-five but built like brick houses.

"If you called us you wouldn't have to throw staplers through windows."

"I did," Paul lied. "Figured you guys forgot about me. It was over two hours ago."

"Well," the officer said. "We didn't get the call. You scared the shit outta that housekeeper."

"I had to get her attention," Paul said. "Was getting stir crazy in here."

"What happened to your face?"

"Excuse me?"

"Looks like you've been in a fight with a grizzly bear."

"Oh," Paul touched the scratches on his face, courtesy of Courtney. "Yeah, I take jiu jitsu. Folks got a little carried away at the dojo the other day."

"Did you call us or the fire department?"

"Just 911," Paul said. "Then the phone line went out. And my cell phone ran out of juice. A comedy of errors."

"Well, you're going to need a new door obviously," the bald officer said looking around.

"Thanks again," Paul said leading the officers out until Russ came running down the hallway.

He was holding hands with Kate as if they were a couple.

"Where is she?" Kate demanded.

"Who?" Paul asked.

Kate ignored the officers and entered the office.

"I'm sorry, man," Russ said. "I can explain. I just. I just needed-"

The officers said nothing, they just looked at each other.

"Where's the girl?" Kate asked Russ.

"He said he had a girl with him," Russ said, looking back into Paul's eyes as if asking for forgiveness of his betrayal. "Said she was drunk and knocked out."

"Anyone else with you?" the black haired officer asked Paul.

"No."

"What the hell are you doing here, Paul?" Kate asked. "You don't work here."

"Really?" both officers said at the same time.

"I can explain," Paul said.

"We're listening-"

"She's got to be around here somewhere," Russ said. Paul grabbed his friend by the arm but Russ broke free.

He looked through the office then made a bee-line for the storage closet.

Russ opened the door before Paul could stop him.

Paul could only close his eyes.

When he opened them, all eyes were on him.

Including the dead eyes of Courtney on the ground.

He didn't bother to run.

If only he had opened the envelope, he thought. He would have seen Russ and his wife together. He would have known not to trust Russ or Kate or anyone.

His father's voice echoed in his head.

"Don't trust anyone. Just cut and run."

www.ingramcontent.com/pod-product-compliance
Lightning Source LLC
Chambersburg PA
CBHW021452150726
47989CB00001B/502